LISTEN

"Good-looking, isn't he?" Gerry commented when she saw me looking at the boy who had just entered the restaurant. He had black hair, only the edges of which were visible under his baseball cap, which was pushed far back on his head.

"Yes," I mumbled. "Who is he?"

"Tim Cortland. Want to meet him?" Gerry waved her hand in Tim's direction, and I panicked.

"No, no!" I looked down and stirred the ice in my glass with my straw. "Not right now."

Gerry looked at me curiously. "What's with you? First you say you want to meet some guys. But when the best-looking guy in Westville comes in, you turn shy. I don't get it."

"I'd like to meet him, just not right now," I said. How could I explain to Gerry how I felt? Tim Cortland was almost *too* gorgeous, and I just wasn't sure I wanted to risk finding out that he was just a regular person.

Bantam Sweet Dreams Romances
Ask your bookseller for the books you have missed

Listen To Your Heart

Marian Caudell

BANTAM BOOKS

TORONTO • NEW YORK • LONDON • SYDNEY • AUCKLAND

RL 5, IL age 11 and up

LISTEN TO YOUR HEART
A Bantam Book / October 1986

*Sweet Dreams and its associated logo are trademarks of
Bantam Books, Inc. Registered in U.S. Patent and Trademark Office
and elsewhere.*

Cover photo by Pat Hill

ISBN 0-553-25727-7

Published simultaneously in the United States and Canada

*Bantam Books are published by Bantam Books, Inc. Its trademark,
consisting of the words "Bantam Books" and the portrayal of a
rooster, is registered in U.S. Patent and Trademark Office and in
other countries. Marca Registrada. Bantam Books, Inc., 666 Fifth
Avenue, New York, New York 10103.*

Printed and bound in Great Britain by Hunt Barnard Printing Ltd.

O   0 9 8 7 6 5 4 3 2 1

—Listen To—
Your Heart

Chapter One

"How do you spell archeology?" asked Cheri.

"A-R-C-H-E-O-L-O-G-Y. Why?" I asked, looking up at her from where I sat cross-legged on the floor, sorting through my albums.

Cheri bit her lower lip and wrote the letters before she answered. "That's what I'm going to major in at college. What did you put down?"

"Nothing." I went back to sorting the records.

"Nothing? You have to put down something, Lori. It says so right here: 'Fill in *all* the blanks.'" Cheri pushed the chair away from the desk and looked at me suspiciously.

"You aren't backing out, are you? I thought it was all settled."

I stood up and stretched, then sat on the edge of my bed. "No, I'm not backing out. I just haven't gotten around to filling out the application," I told her. Cheri had her heart set on going to Broughton College after we graduated the next spring. Her mother had gone there. I didn't have any ties to Broughton, but I'd half promised Cheri I'd go there, too. We had visited the campus once, but I couldn't get excited about college yet. It just didn't seem real.

Cheri and I lived in the same apartment building on Central Park West in New York City. We spent most of our free time together— hanging out in the park during the day and in one of our apartments in the evening.

"We have over six months," I said. "The applications don't have to be in until January."

"But I thought we were going to apply for early-decision."

"OK," I promised. "But even then we have until October. If it'll make you happy, I'll try to fill mine out before I leave. If I don't, I'll do it as soon as I get back. I'll have plenty of time."

"Do you *have* to go?" Cheri asked dejectedly as she sprawled across the foot of my bed.

"You go to Westville every summer. Couldn't you get out of it just this once?"

I shook my head. "Sometimes I wish I could. But my father would be really upset if I didn't come. He counts on my being with him during the summer. Besides, it's only for a couple of months."

For the past eight years, since my parents' divorce, I had shuttled back and forth between two homes. I spent the school year with my mother and stepfather in New York City and summers with my father in Westville, Iowa, where I had lived until I was eight.

"But it's over two months!" Cheri groaned. "I won't have anyone to do stuff with when you're gone."

"What about that family that moved in on the fifth floor?" I asked, trying to cheer her up. "I saw a girl about our age with them the other day. And I heard there's a new boy, too," I added.

"In this building?"

"Of course in this building. I heard my mom asking Mrs. Wright about him the other day. He's her grandson, and he's staying with her for the summer."

"Have you met him?" Cheri asked, brightening a little.

3

"No, I haven't met him, and I have no idea what he looks like. I've been so busy getting my things ready to go that I forgot all about him."

"Yeah, that's because you already have an exciting summer planned," she said.

I laughed. I couldn't help it. "Westville isn't exactly exciting."

"Steve's there," Cheri pointed out.

"Steve's just a friend. Besides, the last time I heard from him was at Christmas when he sent me a card." Steve Raye had lived next door to us in Westville before his family bought a farm and moved to the country.

"Well, you must know a lot of other guys there. And girls, too," Cheri continued.

"Not really," I said truthfully. I knew almost no one. In the eight years since Mom and I had moved to New York, I had lost touch with my old friends. The people I'd known in Westville had either moved away themselves or had changed so much that we weren't friendly anymore. Going back to Westville now wasn't like going home—it was like going to a town I'd visited before but didn't really know.

I was determined to have a fun summer anyway. Instead of spending my days alone, as I had the year before, I had decided to try to

4

meet some new people and find new friends. It wouldn't be easy because I'm shy, but I was going to give it my best effort. Surely not all of the girls my age worked during the day. I hoped that some of them still hung out on the beach. As for boys—well, maybe I'd meet someone interesting, and maybe I wouldn't.

"Hey," I said, turning to Cheri. "I've still got three days left in New York, and there are lots of things we can do together. We can go jogging through the park and see that new Greg Warner movie. Maybe we can even go horseback riding, too. What do you think?"

"The last two sound great, but couldn't we forget the jogging?" Cheri groaned and made a face.

I had to laugh. Even though Cheri usually went with me when I jogged, I knew she hated it. With a lump in my throat, I realized how much I'd miss her. It made me more determined than ever to make new friends in Westville.

Chapter Two

The morning I was to leave for Westville, my mother came into my room to help with the rest of my packing. She picked up my new bikini and held the two pieces out in front of her. "I really like this," she said. "It looks so good on you. And it will look even better with a tan."

She had picked the suit out for me, but it was just what I would have chosen. It was a pretty coral color, just the right shade to set off a tan.

"You don't think it's too daring for Westville, do you?" I asked.

"Of course not," she said. "All the girls wear bikinis." She folded the pieces and put them into my suitcase.

"You haven't been in Westville for a while, Mom," I reminded her. "But it probably won't matter, anyway," I went on. "The city pool is still under construction, and the lake is too far to walk to."

My mother must have caught something in the tone of my voice. There was a concerned look in her eyes as she turned to me.

"What's wrong, Lori? Don't you want to go? You've always looked forward to spending the summer with your father."

"Of course I want to go," I assured her. "It's just that last summer was pretty boring. There wasn't much for me to do during the day while Dad was at work. But don't worry. I'm going to make sure this year is different."

"Good. Your father would be terribly disappointed if you didn't show up."

"Mom! Are you kidding? I'd never think of not going!" I reassured her. My parents were very conscientious about making sure I spent time with both of them, and I loved them for it. I would have been miserable if they had fought and argued over custody the way some divorced parents do.

"Remember, you have your license now, too," Mom continued. "I'm sure your father will let you drive his car. You can go to the lake anytime you want."

I nodded. "At least on days when he doesn't need his car."

Mom closed my suitcase and snapped it shut. Then she sat on the edge of my bed and folded her hands in her lap. "Lori—" she began tentatively.

"Yes?" I asked, expecting the usual reminders to keep my room clean, get enough sleep, and help my dad out around the house. I picked up my blow-dryer and began to wrap the cord around it.

"Have you thought any more about college?" she asked.

"What about it, Mom?" I placed the blow-dryer in my suitcase on top of an assortment of bottles and brushes.

"Have you decided where you want to go yet?"

I must have looked as puzzled as I felt because she went on, "I don't mean to rush you. There's plenty of time."

"You know Cheri wants me to go to Broughton with her," I said. "I've got an application, but I haven't filled it out yet."

I could tell that my mother wanted to say something but didn't quite know how to start.

"Is it the money?" I asked anxiously. "I could go to City College instead. I could even live at home if it would help."

"No, dear, it isn't that. I was just thinking. Would you want to go to Iowa State or the University of Iowa? I'm sure your father would like it if you did. Then we'd just reverse our arrangement. You'd be with him in the winter and here in the summer." She was running her sentences together, and I knew she had been thinking about it for some time.

"I don't know, Mom," I said, frowning. "It never occurred to me that I could go to college in Iowa."

"It was just a thought," Mom said gently. "Well, you'd better finish packing. We don't have much time before we leave for the airport." She got up, smoothed her skirt, and added, "You'll give it some thought, won't you?"

"Sure, Mom," I said. "I'll think about it."

My stepfather, Casey, and my mom drove me to the airport. When we pulled up outside the terminal, we all got out of the car, and Casey took my suitcases out of the trunk. "I'll carry them in for you," he said.

"Oh, that's OK, thanks," I said. "I think I

can manage." I gave them each a kiss, then said to my mom, "I'll call you from Dad's."

They drove away, and I went inside the terminal. I checked my suitcases, got my boarding pass and seat assignment, and looked at my watch. I still had half an hour—plenty of time to pick out some good books. I headed for the newsstand.

Right away I spotted two novels by my favorite author. I picked those up and glanced at the titles in the next row. Some of them sounded interesting, too.

I started to pick up one of them and then looked down uncertainly at the two books I already had. If I began the summer on the front porch with a book, I just might spend the entire time there. Well, I wasn't going to forget my resolution. I turned away from the book rack, paid for the two books I had picked out, and hurried to my gate.

Chapter Three

My dad met me at the airport in Des Moines. He gave me a big bear hug. Then he stood back and looked at me, his hands on my shoulders. "You're more beautiful than ever," he said.

"You're prejudiced," I replied, laughing to hide my embarrassment. It had always bothered me when someone, even my parents, told me I was pretty. I never knew what to say. I knew I wasn't ugly, but I certainly didn't think I was beautiful, either. I had always thought my wide-set eyes and high cheekbones made my face look a little too broad. And I wished I had my mother's curly, sun-streaked hair. Instead, I had inherited my dad's hair—dark and very straight.

"Of course I'm prejudiced," he said, laughing along with me. "Seriously, though, you do look great." He tilted my chin up with his hand and studied me closely. "You look a little older, a little more mature."

"Well, you don't," I countered. "Aren't you ever going to get any gray hair? Or do you dye it?"

A look of horror passed over his face. "Dye my hair? Lori, people in Westville do not dye their hair."

"I guess you're right," I agreed. "What would everyone think?"

We walked arm in arm over to the baggage area. As Dad reached for my suitcases, I noticed that there was something different about him. I couldn't tell exactly what it was. Tall, slim, and good-looking, he was dressed casually in a short-sleeved sport shirt and sharply creased gray trousers. He wore black loafers.

"New shoes?" I asked. "I don't think I've ever seen you wearing loafers before."

"Yes, as a matter of fact they are new. What do you think?"

"They look great," I said. It wasn't the shoes that made him seem different, though. It was something else, but I still couldn't figure out what it was.

When we got to the parking lot, I looked around for our old car. "Where's the car?" I finally asked.

"You're standing right beside it," Dad said, grinning.

"This?" I asked with disbelief. We had stopped in front of a gleaming blue Toyota.

"Don't you like it?" He sounded anxious.

"It's gorgeous! When did you get it? How come you didn't tell me?"

"I wanted it to be a surprise. There are more surprises, too, but you won't see them until we get home." He unlocked the trunk and stowed my suitcases while I walked around the car, admiring it.

"Here, catch!" Dad threw the keys to me. "You drive."

"Me?"

"Yes, you. If you're going to be driving it all summer, you might as well start getting used to it."

After I slid behind the wheel and adjusted the seat, I looked over the dash. "Is that what I think it is?" I asked, pointing just below the radio.

Dad pushed the little swinging door in.

13

"Yes. A tape deck. But I don't think I have any tapes you'd like. I figured you might want to pick some out yourself. It will give you something to do."

A wave of guilt swept over me. He knew how bored I'd been last summer, and he was already worried that this summer would be as bad.

I started the engine and eased away from the other cars. As we left Des Moines behind, Dad looked over at me and said, "It's good to have my best girl back home."

"It's good to be home," I said sincerely. After all, Westville was just as much my home as New York was, even if it didn't always feel that way.

We were both quiet during the drive home. My dad had such a preoccupied look on his face that I couldn't help but wonder what he was thinking about.

"Take it easy here," Dad said as I started around the corner onto our street.

"What have you done to the house?" I shrieked when I turned into the driveway. "That *is* it, isn't it?"

I almost didn't recognize the house I had lived in for years. The front porch was gone, the clapboard siding had been replaced with redwood panels, and evergreens had been planted around the front door. The house had taken on a rustic appearance.

"Wait until you see the inside," he said with pride. "You won't recognize the old place! Come on, we'll get your bags later."

The changes he had made on the inside were even more dramatic than those on the outside. All of the old, dark, overstuffed chairs and the odd assortment of end tables were gone. Two white love seats faced each other in front of the brick fireplace with its new oak mantel. Sheer blue curtains, which matched the plush carpeting, replaced the heavy drapes that had been there before. A fig tree stood in one corner, where it caught the light coming in through the windows.

The kitchen, too, had been transformed. There were new cabinets, built-in appliances— including a microwave oven—and several hanging plants. The whole room was bright and airy looking.

"I'll bet Mrs. Irman likes this," I said. Mrs. Irman was the lady who came in to clean, wash, and cook for my father.

"You know Mrs. Irman," said Dad. "She complains that it's too modern for her. I think she likes the new garden better, though." He opened a sliding door that I hadn't even noticed and led me out onto a new redwood deck. There were a gas grill, picnic table, and padded lounge chairs on it. The deck curved around three large trees, which shaded it completely. Suspended from a wooden beam on one side of the deck hung our old porch swing. I had spent many, many hours on that old, slotted wooden swing. A new flowered seat cushion stretched across it.

"You kept it!" I cried, dashing over to sit down. Grinning, I quipped, "Where's the pool?"

Dad grinned as he sat down beside me. "I'm afraid the pool will have to wait a while. *All* of that money at the bank isn't mine, you know."

"I'm only kidding, Dad. It's beautiful. So peaceful and private."

"It's a nice place to invite friends," he said, glancing toward the grill and table. "For some reason, food always tastes better when it's cooked outside. Of course, we'll have to do our own cooking out here. I don't think I can get Mrs. Irman to come in for that."

"Did you do all of this yourself—plan it all, I mean?"

"No. A friend helped me."

Before I had time to ask him who the friend

was, he rushed on, "Now for the pièce de résistance. Your room."

"You even did my room over? But what for? This is the last summer I'll—I'll get to use it much," I finished lamely. I'd started to say, "the last summer I'll be here," but I didn't want to dampen Dad's enthusiasm. To hide my embarrassment, I jumped up and ran into the house. "It's still in the same place, isn't it?" I called back over my shoulder.

When I opened the door to my room, I gasped with delight. The whole room was done in lavender and white. At first I thought the furniture was all new, but then I saw it was the same high, four-poster bed. Now it had a ruffled canopy that matched new curtains. I'd never seen anything like it before, except in decorating magazines.

Dad had even gotten a small white step stool so I could get up onto the huge bed more easily. I stepped up, sat on the bed, and ran my hand over the lavender spread, grinning speechlessly at my dad.

"I remembered that purple is your favorite color," Dad said from the doorway. "How do you like the dresser and chest?"

They had belonged to my great-grand-mother, but they had been completely

17

refinished. Both shone with a patina that only a great deal of hand rubbing could have achieved.

"You spent an awful lot of time on them," I said with awe.

"You're worth it." Dad paused as if he were about to add something else. I looked at him expectantly. He stood there for a second and then said, "Let's get your suitcases so you can unpack. Mrs. Irman left a casserole in the refrigerator. I'll stick it in the oven while you get settled in."

I hopped off the bed. "Let's eat on the deck," I said. If my dad had something to tell me, it would have to wait until dinner.

Chapter Four

I opened a couple of my suitcases, but I didn't unpack very much. I was too anxious to get back outside. There would be plenty of time to hang everything up later that night or the next day. But I did take time to brush my hair. When I laid the brush on the dresser, I saw my grandmother's hand mirror lying there as it had every summer. Somehow, it made me feel that this strange but beautiful room really was mine.

In my excitement I almost forgot to call my mom. We had a short conversation, and I saved any mention of the "new" house for a letter. Then I went out to set the table. As soon as we had finished eating, we loaded the dishes into the new dishwasher and went back outside.

"Let's sit on the swing for a while," Dad said. "Unless you have something you want to do."

"After that delicious dinner, I'm too full to do anything but sit," I said.

For several minutes neither of us said anything. We listened to the creak of the chains as the swing moved gently back and forth. I finally broke the silence. "I guess all swings creak, huh?"

"This one always has. It could also stand a new coat of paint. I thought about throwing it away and buying a new one, but at the last minute I got sentimental and had it hung out here."

"I'm glad you did."

"It's a good place just to sit and talk, too. In fact, your mother and I were sitting on this very swing when I asked her to marry me. It was on the porch at Nana's house back then, of course."

"I remember." I had heard the story before, but it had always delighted me. How romantic and old-fashioned! I imagined the full moon, the crickets chirping above the squeak of the chain, and the two young lovers sitting quietly, planning their future.

Maybe that would be the way it would happen to me. I hoped so. But I couldn't picture who would be sitting next to me. I was so lost in my daydreams that I didn't realize my dad had spoken.

"What?" I asked.

"I said there's another surprise I haven't told you about yet."

"Another?"

"Yes. There's someone I'd like you to meet."

"Who?" I asked.

"A very dear friend of mine," Dad said, hesitating. "Cathy Wellman."

"Oh?" The name sounded vaguely familiar.

"You don't have to meet her right away," Dad added hastily. "In fact, she isn't even in town right now—she's visiting her sister. Cathy teaches home economics at the high school. I met her last winter. Since then we've been seeing a lot of each other." He laughed a little nervously. "Anyway, I didn't want Mrs. Irman to mention Cathy's name and have you wonder who she was."

Then I knew what it was that was different about my father. It wasn't his clothes at all. It was a new confidence. Perhaps it was because of Cathy.

"What's she like?" I asked.

"She's—well, I'd rather not say. I'd rather have you just meet her."

"Do you have any pictures of her?"

"Yes, but they don't do her justice. Photographs never capture the real person, anyway. And I'd like you to get to know Cathy a little before you form an opinion."

I was silent for a moment. Then, quietly, I said, "She's the friend who helped you redo the house, isn't she?"

"Yes."

"She has very good taste." I wanted to say something more encouraging, so I added, "I'm sure I'll like her, Dad."

I could hear him sigh in the darkness. I wondered if he was going to marry Cathy. After all, Mom had remarried, and Dad was bound to, too.

"When will I meet her?" I asked a little too brightly.

"In a few days," he replied. "Now, you've had a long day, haven't you?"

As if on cue, I yawned. I was more tired than I had realized. We said good night to each other, and I went to my room.

When I got into bed, I found I was too keyed up to sleep. I lay awake for a long time, thinking. The adjustment had been hard when my mother had married Casey. Even though I had grown to love him, I still remembered those difficult days in the beginning. Now I had the feeling it was starting all over again.

Maybe my dad *wasn't* planning to marry Cathy. It seemed likely, though. With all of the work they had done on the house, I was sure Cathy had become a permanent part of my father's life.

My fingers brushed against the bedspread in the darkness. I wondered how much of the redecorating she had done and why she'd bothered. Was it a bribe? I knew my dad would never stoop to such tricks, but I didn't know how Cathy might act. I hoped at least the color had been my father's idea.

Suddenly I was very angry with myself. What was wrong with me? Was I jealous? Why shouldn't my father date someone once in a while? He was almost forty, but he was still very good-looking. And he had probably been very lonely. Feeling a bit better, I flipped on the bedside light. Whenever I was worried, I liked to read in bed.

"Lori?" Dad called. "Are you all right?"

"I'm fine," I called through the door. "I just couldn't sleep."

"See you in the morning, honey."

"OK, Dad. Good night," I called. That night even reading wouldn't help. I lay back down with the light on and tried to think of other things—Cheri, Broughton, horseback riding in Central Park, anything. It was well after midnight when I finally, fitfully, dropped off to sleep.

Chapter Five

The light was still on when I woke up. For a second I didn't know where I was. Then I remembered. The sun was streaming through the window, and I knew it must be late.

I looked over at the dresser to see what time it was, but the clock wasn't there. An old windup clock, which ticked very loudly, had been on my bedside table for years. With a little feeling of triumph, I thought that Cathy wasn't perfect. She had forgotten to put the alarm clock back.

Once out of bed, I looked at my watch on the dresser. It was already eleven-thirty! I must have been really exhausted. I slipped a cotton robe over my nightgown and went down to the kitchen to see if Mrs. Irman was still there.

I found her at the breakfast table, her purse on her lap as if she were trying to remember something. Her gray eyes lit up when she saw me.

"Lori, welcome home," she said with a warm smile. "You're looking wonderful, as always."

Mrs. Irman was a kind woman. With her soft, round figure and silvery hair, she seemed more like an old aunt than an employee.

"It's good to see you, too," I said. "And that casserole was delicious. We ate every bit of it."

"I noticed." There was a hint of pride in her voice. "I've left some potato salad and deviled eggs in the fridge for you. And there are cold cuts, too. Your father said not to fix anything else because he wants to cook on that thing out there tonight." She nodded toward the grill. "And he left you a note on the counter. I'd best be going now." She rose and started toward the living room.

Lying on top of the note was a car key attached to a Lucite triangle with an *L* on it. I heard the front door close as I read, "Meet me for lunch. Same time, same place. Love, Dad."

The same time meant twelve o'clock. I rushed back upstairs and dressed in record time.

I could have gotten to the bank where my

father worked almost as quickly by walking as by driving. But I couldn't resist the lure of the new car. *Next time I'll walk*, I promised myself.

My dad was sitting at his desk looking at his watch when I walked into his office. "Oversleep?" he asked, smiling.

"A little," I answered sheepishly.

"Well, let's get some lunch—or in your case, breakfast."

We went across the street to Neal's Lunchroom. It wasn't a fancy place, but it was neat and clean. The food was always good and the hamburgers were enormous. Several people greeted Dad as we came in. A few people recognized me and called out hellos.

"What do you have planned for the rest of the day?" Dad asked after we had ordered. "Or haven't you been up long enough to plan anything?"

"Not really," I said. "Maybe I'll sit in the swing and read. I brought a couple of books with me."

"Why don't you drive down to the lake for a swim? That's where most of the young people go. There's a season pass in the glove compartment of the car." He said it very casually, but he didn't look at me as he spoke.

I had the feeling that he was afraid I'd be mad. He knew I didn't like to be fussed over. But getting a pass for me was sweet.

"Thanks, Dad. I will." I would have to start meeting people sometime, and there was no point in putting it off. I knew that the longer I waited, the more unsure of myself I would feel.

After we ate I drove around town to see if anything had changed. The only thing I noticed was a new softball field next to the high school. *That's a blessing*, I thought. The bleachers by the old field out back were about to fall down.

Then I drove toward the lake in the state park, going slowly along the tree-lined road until I came to the beach area. I hadn't brought my bathing suit, but I decided to stop for a moment on the road to look at the lake. I could see all the way across it to the woods on the far shore. It was a lovely, peaceful scene. Since there were no cars behind me, I switched off the engine. Draping my arms around the steering wheel, I rested my chin on my hands and gazed across the water.

I don't know how long I sat there, but it must have been awhile. I didn't hear the car pull up behind me. Suddenly a deep male voice, tinged with amusement, said right beside me, "It's a pretty view, but you could see it just as well if you'd pull your car in the parking lot instead of stopping in the middle of the road."

I turned at the sound of his voice and came face to face with the most handsome boy I'd ever seen, with warm brown eyes and dark hair. I just stared at him for a moment. Then I glanced quickly in the rearview mirror. There were three cars lined up behind me, patiently waiting for me to move.

Embarrassed, I started the engine and stepped on the gas. The motor roared, but the car didn't budge.

"You might try putting it in gear," the boy said.

"I can drive!" I answered stiffly, feeling my face begin to burn. It was the first time I had spoken.

I could hear his amused laughter as I shifted into drive and edged over to the side of the road to make a right turn. I couldn't have acted more like a fool if I'd tried.

He got back in his car and followed me through the park until we came to the campground. I drove past it; he turned into it. I was alone on the road.

Taking a deep breath, I tried to calm my

racing heart. But I couldn't forget his teasing smile or the kindness in his eyes. If I saw him again, I thought, I wouldn't be able to face him. Then again, if I didn't see him, I'd never get another glimpse of the most gorgeous boy in the world.

When I got back to the house, I finished unpacking and got all my things in order. Then I wandered around the house and garden, once more admiring the changes.

About four o'clock I looked up Steve Raye's number in the phone book. I dialed it and let the phone ring eight times. *Maybe it's just as well,* I thought, when no one answered. Steve probably had a girlfriend. He would only feel awkward if I called him. I wished that I'd been friendlier last summer, that there was someone else I could call. A picture of the boy at the lake flashed through my mind as I left the room.

The next day I drove back to the lake. After parking I walked down to the bathhouse and paused at the top of the long flight of steps leading down to the beach itself. There were a lot of people already there.

I wasn't interested in family types, so I quickly passed over them as I searched for a group of girls, even one or two, who looked about my age. Although I didn't want to admit it, I knew I was also looking for the boy from the parking lot.

I was about to give up when three girls came splashing out of the water and flopped down on a blanket right in front of the steps. Clutching my towel a little tighter and strengthening my resolve, I headed in their direction.

"Hi," I said to them. For a minute I didn't think they heard me because no one looked up.

I felt so awkward! Just as I was about to go by and pretend I hadn't said anything, one of them said, "Hi. Hey, you're Mr. Nichols's daughter, aren't you?" She was slightly over-weight, with copper red hair.

"Yes," I said, relieved and surprised. "How did you know?"

"I've seen you around," she said, shrugging.

I wondered briefly why they had never spoken to me if they knew who I was. "I'm Lori," I said.

"I'm Gerry," the redhead said. "And this is Rosemary. And Bette." She indicated the other two, who nodded stiffly. They all looked as if they weren't sure why I was standing there or what I wanted.

"How's the water?" I asked, desperate for something to say.

"Wet," said Gerry solemnly. Rosemary and Bette broke up, and I smiled sheepishly, feeling as if I were the butt of a joke.

"Wet and cold," said Rosemary finally. "Want to sit down?" She waved vaguely toward one end of their blanket, and I sat down gratefully.

"I guess you're here to spend the summer with your father," said Bette.

"Yes," I answered. Then we were silent. I couldn't think of anything else to say.

Finally Bette mumbled, "I'm tired," and stretched out on her stomach. Rosemary did the same. Gerry gave me an embarrassed glance, then quickly looked away, squinting into the sun.

I sat there as long as I could stand it, then said to no one in particular, "I think I'll go swimming."

I could feel Gerry's eyes on me as I ran into the lake. I dived under a wave; the water felt wonderful. I swam to the pier, climbed on to it, then did a back dive. I practiced all the routines I could remember from my high-school synchronized swim team. Our team, the Dolphins, would be back in competition shortly after school started, and I wanted to keep in shape.

After a while I began to get tired, so I treaded water and glanced back toward the beach. Gerry, Rosemary, and Bette were looking at me. Gerry said something to them, and they all laughed. My stomach contracted into one big, hard knot. Their laughter hurt, but it also made me angry. What right did they have to laugh at me? What had I done except try to be friendly?

With a strong kick, I dived under the water and swam toward the pier. When I pulled myself up over the side and looked around, they were picking up their things. I waited until they had enough time to get out of the parking lot before I went back to get my own things. *There are other girls in Westville,* I told myself. *And not all of them can be as rude and cruel as those three.*

Chapter Six

One morning a few days after that terrible day at the beach, Dad told me that Cathy was back in Westville. He had made plans for the three of us to go out to dinner that night. I was a nervous wreck for the rest of the day. Finally evening came, and we drove over to her house to meet her.

My first thought when I saw her was that she looked much too young to be a teacher. She was about five feet four and had soft brown hair that curled gently just below her ears. She was thin, almost too thin, and she moved gracefully—more, I thought, like a dancer than a home ec teacher.

"Hi, Lori," she said as she climbed into the backseat. "I'm Cathy."

Her greeting threw me off guard. I had expected the introductions to be awkward. But Cathy acted as if she had known me all my life.

"Everything all right with Emily?" Dad asked her.

"That's my sister," Cathy said to me. "Yes, John, she's fine."

"Cathy has a new nephew," my father explained. I knew they were just trying to include me in their conversation, but their efforts made it clear how much they knew about each other's lives.

I should have offered to ride in the backseat and let Cathy sit in the front, but I hadn't. It had been my childish way of saying, "I'm first." I sank lower in my seat and sat quietly for the rest of the ride.

At the restaurant the hostess led us across the dining room toward a booth. I wondered whether my dad would sit next to me or Cathy. I hoped he'd sit with me; if he didn't, I would feel as if I were on the witness stand.

I had worried in vain. When we got to the booth, Cathy asked the hostess if we could have the small round table in the corner instead. We all sat facing one another.

"Well, Lori," Cathy began in a friendly voice,

"have you decided where you want to go to college yet?"

Then she started asking me about my life—school, the junior prom, New York. She even asked about Cheri. I began to suspect that she had read my letters. She never started her sentences with, "Your father told me," or "Your father said."

The more questions she asked, the more resentful I became. She had no right to read my letters. I answered her questions in short, angry tones. I knew I was being deliberately difficult, but I was unable to stop myself.

Cathy didn't seem to notice. Her expression remained warm and friendly. I glanced sideways at my father, hoping he would understand how I felt. I was surprised to find him looking at me with love and pride in his eyes.

I knew then that if he had shared my letters with Cathy, it was because he was proud of me. Maybe it would be easier to try to like Cathy. I decided to relax and try to be nice.

We didn't talk much after our food came. As I ate in silence, it occurred to me that Cathy had been very tactful. Her request for the round table instead of a booth showed that she didn't want me to feel that she was going to come between my father and me.

It reminded me of the first time I met Casey. He, too, had known a lot about me, although I knew almost nothing about him. I also remembered how I'd been so afraid I wouldn't be loved and accepted by him. It wasn't until I was older that Casey told me he'd had the same fears about me.

A rush of shame swept over me. I was angry at myself for the unkind thoughts I had had about Cathy. She was probably just as nervous as I was, and I'd only made things worse.

The silence soon became uncomfortable, and I knew it was up to me to break it. Cathy hadn't mentioned the house. I was sure that she must have wondered what I thought about it.

"I love my room, especially the canopy," I commented.

It was the right thing to say. I could feel my father relax as Cathy's smile lit up her whole face. She practically glowed.

"I was a little worried about the ruffles and the canopy," she admitted. "John told me your favorite color was lavender, but I was afraid you might think ruffles were too little-girlish."

"It's perfect," I said with conviction. "The only thing I miss is my old alarm clock. Dad says it ticks loud enough for him to hear in his room, but I'm kind of attached to it."

Cathy looked so stricken that I added hastily, "It doesn't really matter, though."

"I forgot all about the clock," Dad confessed. "The alarm wouldn't ring, so I took it to the jeweler's to be repaired. I guess it's still there."

"It never worked," I said with a sheepish grin.

My dad and Cathy looked so confused that I had to explain. "That's what I liked about it. I always set the alarm every night, but it never rang. That way I always had an excuse to sleep late."

Cathy and my father both began to laugh. I joined in and the tension was broken.

Later when we left the restaurant, I hurried ahead and climbed into the backseat. Cathy had shown me that she wouldn't try to take my place. Now it was my turn to show Cathy that I wouldn't try to take hers.

Chapter Seven

The clatter of dishes woke me the next morning. Slipping on my robe, I went downstairs and started across the living room. I could see Cathy through the front window. She was climbing out of a small, red sports car. Standing astride a bicycle next to the car was Gerry, the chunky girl I had met at the beach. She had a very unhappy look on her face.

I turned away from the window and went into the kitchen.

"Hi, Mrs. Irman," I said, taking a piece of bread out of the bread drawer. I put the bread in the toaster and pushed the start button.

"Good morning, Lori. You're up early today."

I heard the front door open and close, and I raised my voice. "I have a lot to do today. I wanted to get started early." Actually, I had nothing planned. I was afraid Cathy would invite me to come along with her if she knew I didn't have anything to do.

"Lori!" Cathy stood alone in the kitchen doorway. "I didn't expect you up yet." She turned to Mrs. Irman. "How are you today, Mrs. Irman? Have you tried the microwave yet?"

"No, those things cook too fast. Makes me feel as though I haven't done a thorough job."

Cathy laughed. "I know what you mean. It's nice to sit down and read the paper while dinner is in the oven. But microwaves are great time-savers, especially when you work all day."

Mrs. Irman ignored that. "What about that tree in the living room? Do you want me to water it?" she asked. I could tell that Mrs. Irman didn't completely approve of having a tree indoors.

"It's OK," said Cathy. "I checked it on the way in." Turning to me, she reached into her tote bag. "I brought your clock by." She produced the old, round alarm clock. "I'm afraid it works now. The jeweler said it's such an old model that he didn't have any new parts for it, but he found some old ones in his spare parts collection. I didn't have the heart to tell him to take them back out." She grinned at me. "I guess you'll just have to pretend that you set it."

"Thanks," I said, smiling. I took the clock from her.

"Well, I have to run. I'm meeting some of the girls at school today. I'll see you later," she said. She was gone before I had a chance to say anything else.

I buttered my toast, poured myself a glass of orange juice, and sat down to eat.

"Lori?" asked Mrs. Irman after I had finished eating, "are you OK?"

"Sure," I said. "Why?"

"You said you were in a big rush, but you've just been sitting there, staring into space." She added in a soft, kind tone, "If you're worried about Miss Wellman, she's a fine young lady, Lori. I'm sure you'll get along with her once you get to know her."

"Oh, I do like her," I insisted. "It's not that. I was just thinking about all the things I want to do today."

"Well, you won't get anything done just sitting there."

"You're right," I agreed. Jumping up, I picked up the clock and hurried out of the kitchen.

After I made my bed and took a shower, I picked out a pair of blue shorts and a white V-neck T-shirt. Then I got into the car and drove to the new mall, where I spent the day. I bought some tapes, had lunch, saw a movie, and window-shopped for a while. As I headed home, I decided the change of scene had been good for me.

When I rounded the corner onto Maple Street, I saw Cathy's little red car parked in front of our house.

"Lori?" my dad called from the patio as I closed the front door. "Is that you?"

"Yes," I called back. "I'll be out in a few minutes. I have some things to put away."

"There's no hurry," he said. "We weren't going to put the steaks on until you got here, anyway."

I took my time. Through my bedroom window, I could see my father and Cathy sitting on the swing. They were drinking iced tea and talking quietly. I was sure they would like to spend at least part of the evening alone.

I decided to wear my sleeveless yellow dress with the scoop neck and ruffles around the bottom. Dad and Cathy would be sure to think that I planned on going out. Then I could leave right after dinner, and they could have the evening to themselves. I didn't know where I'd go, but I knew I'd figure something out.

I curled the ends of my hair under with my curling iron and applied some light makeup. Then I went downstairs.

"You look marvelous," Cathy said when I joined them on the deck. "I wish I could tan the way you do. All I do is burn and then peel."

"It's my Indian heritage," I answered solemnly.

"Really?" Cathy looked questioningly at my father.

Dad grinned and explained. "It's a family joke. When Lori was a little girl, she used to get so brown in the summer that her mother and I called her our little Indian." Then he looked at me, nodding with approval at my dress. "Is all this for our benefit, or do you have a date?"

"No," I said honestly. "But I thought I might walk downtown, maybe to Baker's, and see who's there."

Cathy and I talked while Dad grilled the steaks. After we finished eating, I pushed my chair back and let out a contented sigh. "The steaks were delicious, Dad," I said. "I was really famished." I got up, picked up my plate, and started inside.

"Just leave the dishes here, Lori," Cathy offered. "We can take them in later. You'd better get going if you're going to meet anyone. I don't think the kids hang out at Baker's very late in the summer."

"OK. See you later." I went inside, picked up my purse, and slipped out the front door.

Chapter Eight

Cathy was right about the kids not staying inside in the summer. When I got to Baker's, it looked closed. But the front door was open, so I went inside. The place was deserted. The only people there were old Mr. Baker, who was standing behind the soda fountain, and a guy playing a video game in the back.

The video machines took up the whole back wall. They had been put in two summers before. The wall opposite the counter had built-in booths, and there were tables in the middle. *Well*, I thought, *as long as I'm here, I might as well have a soda and try to kill some time.* I slipped onto a stool at the counter. *Maybe, if I'm lucky, the guy from the park will come in.*

While Mr. Baker was getting my soda, I looked again at the guy in the back. He looked familiar, but I couldn't figure out who he was. Then he turned sideways, and I got a better look at him. It was Steve! Steve Raye! He had grown so much since I'd seen him that I hadn't recognized him.

He was concentrating so hard on his game that he hadn't noticed me come into the restaurant. I waited eagerly for him to finish, keeping one eye on him as I sipped at my soda. Finally he turned around and started for the front door.

As he approached me, I turned around on the stool and said, "Steve? Hi—"

Steve looked at me with surprise, nodded, and walked right on past me.

The rest of my words died in my throat—I could have cried. Turning back toward the counter, I tipped my head down and looked into my empty glass, thankful that Mr. Baker was polishing the tables in the back of the room. My face burned with embarrassment. Then I heard Steve's voice. "Lori Nichols!"

I looked back in his direction. Steve stood there with a big smile lighting up his tanned face. Then he sat down on the stool next to me.

"Lori!" he said again, looking me up and down. "I'm sorry, I didn't recognize you. You've changed so much."

"I guess I have," I said shyly.

"Have you been here long?" he asked.

"About fifteen minutes," I said. I wanted the conversation to last as long as possible. I hadn't realized how much I had missed talking to someone my own age.

"I mean in Westville," Steve said. "What have you been doing with yourself?"

"Swimming and reading, mostly," I said. "I just got here, actually. Do you go out to the lake very often?" I knew he didn't, or I would have seen him the couple of times I had gone.

"Not really. I don't have time. There's too much work to do on the farm. I don't even get into town very often."

"Oh," I said, thinking how frivolous I must have sounded. "I guess you don't have much free time, huh?"

"Not for the next few weeks, anyway." Steve spread his hands open. Even in the muted light, I could see that they were hard and callused.

"That's too bad," I said. "I'll bet they could really use you on one of the softball teams. You look as if you could hit a lot of home runs."

"I'd like to play, but I don't have the time right now. In fact, I've got to get going. We're putting up hay tonight." He slid off the stool. "Maybe we can get together sometime."

"Sure." I smiled brightly to hide my disappointment. Then I watched him through the window as he got on a motorcycle and sped away. He had seemed truly glad to see me. But if he had to farm all day and into the night, he obviously wasn't going to have much time for me.

I left Baker's and started toward home. It was still early, so I walked past the house and over to the softball field. A bunch of kids were gathered along the benches watching. They were all dressed in shorts and T-shirts, and I felt so overdressed that I didn't even stop. I just walked on by as if I had somewhere important to go.

After walking around aimlessly for a while, I went back home and joined my father and Cathy on the deck.

"Did you have a good time, honey?" Dad asked. "You're in pretty early."

"I met Steve Raye," I said, "but he had to get back to the farm before dark to help put up the rest of the hay."

"So that's why you were in such a hurry,"

said Cathy. "I don't know Steve very well, but he's quite popular in school. He seems like a very nice boy."

"He is," I said. I knew they thought we'd had a date. I felt guilty about letting them believe a lie. But I also didn't want them worrying about me and my social life. It was probably better not to tell them.

"Listen, since tomorrow's Wednesday and the bank will be closed," my dad said suddenly, "how about going over to the new mall for the day? We could look around, go somewhere for dinner, and even go to a movie if you'd like." He looked questioningly from Cathy to me. I decided not to tell him that I'd been to the mall already.

"I'd love to," said Cathy. "But I couldn't leave until after noon. I'm meeting with some girls in the morning to help them with their projects for the fair."

"Couldn't you postpone it until Thursday?" my dad asked.

Cathy shook her head. "I've already put it off once. Some of the girls don't have sewing machines at home. I promised them that I'd open the home ec room at school so they could finish the dresses they're making."

"I'd forgotten about the Four-H fair," Dad said. "Are they going to be ready for it?"

"I think so," Cathy replied. "The only one I'm concerned about is Gerry Ruttman." Cathy went on to explain that Gerry had been having a hard time finding a pattern that fit and wasn't too difficult, either.

Dad looked thoughtful. "Well, we could leave in the afternoon. I thought if we went early, we could get back in time for Lori to meet Steve if she wanted to?" He looked over at me questioningly.

"Steve?" I asked stupidly as if I'd never heard the name before. "No, that's OK," I finally managed to say. "I don't have any plans to meet Steve." Then I turned to Cathy.

"The girl you were talking to outside this morning—that was Gerry, wasn't it?"

"Yes. Do you know her?" Cathy asked. "Why didn't you come out?"

"I-I wasn't dressed." I stammered a little. "And I don't really know her very well," I added. "I saw her at the lake the other day with a couple of girls."

Cathy nodded, then sighed. "That was Gerry, all right. She practically lives at that lake. That's where she would have been today if I hadn't run into her in front of your house

50

this morning. She wasn't very happy about spending the whole day cutting out and pinning her new pattern."

"Why did she enter the dressmaking competition if she doesn't like to sew?"

"She failed home ec this past spring because she didn't get her last project done. I told her that I'd pass her if she completed an outfit for the fair. But at the rate she's going, I'm not sure she's going to make it."

"Well," Dad said, "since you'll be free in the afternoon and Lori doesn't have any plans for tomorrow night, let's take off about one. OK?"

Cathy and I both agreed. With that settled, I excused myself and went upstairs.

Chapter Nine

The next morning I went downstairs just as my dad was finishing breakfast. I poured myself a glass of orange juice and sat down at the kitchen table across from him.

"I have a few errands to run this morning, and I want to stop in at the office," he said. "There's a little paperwork I've been putting off, but I'll be back before noon. If you aren't too busy, could you hose off the deck?"

"Sure," I said, thankful to have anything useful to do. He got up, gave me a quick kiss, and then left. As soon as I had finished eating, I put on my bathing suit and got the hose out. Most of the yard was shaded, but it was still pretty hot outside. When I got far enough away from the house, I turned the hose straight up in the air and let the water fall on me like a shower.

I was thinking how good it felt when Mrs. Irman stepped out of the kitchen and called to me, "Telephone, Lori."

I laid the hose down. Could Steve be calling me? I wondered. No, it couldn't be him. It was probably Dad.

Wiping my feet on the towel I had brought outside with me, I went through the kitchen and picked up the phone. "Hello."

"Lori?" It was Cathy. "Hi. Mrs. Irman said your dad is out and—" She paused as if she didn't know what to say next.

"He'll be back before noon," I said. "He's just running a few errands."

"I hate to bother you, but"—she hesitated—"would you do me a favor?"

"Sure."

"I need my pinking shears. The ones here are so dull they won't cut anything. Would you go to my house, get mine, and bring them over? I'd go myself, but I'm not authorized to leave these girls alone in the home ec room."

"That's OK. I'd be glad to get them," I told her.

"Good. I don't think you'll have any trouble

finding them. My house is really only one big room. My sewing machine is on the right as you go through the front door. Oh, and the house isn't locked, so you won't need a key," she said. Then she explained to me how to find the home ec room.

"I'll be right over with them," I said. After I hung up, I wished that I had asked her to meet me at the door so I wouldn't have to go inside.

"I've got to go out for a while, Mrs. Irman," I called through the kitchen doorway. "I'll finish the deck when I get back."

Rushing up to my room, I picked out a flowered wraparound skirt and tied it around my waist. Over it, I threw on a white cotton T-shirt. My bathing suit was still wet underneath my clothes, but I didn't have time to change. I brushed out my hair and pulled it back in a ponytail. Slipping into some sandals, I ran down the stairs.

With my car keys in my hand, I headed for the garage, only to find it empty. *Of course,* I thought. *Dad has the car today.* I had forgotten about that. I wondered if my bicycle still worked. The old ten-speed my father had gotten me five years before hung on brackets on the garage wall. I eyed it doubtfully. I pushed the back tire in—all the way—to the rim. I checked the front tire, and it was also flat.

Well, I thought, *Cathy's house isn't that far away.* I set off on foot. A few minutes later I arrived at the tiny house. It felt strange to walk up to the front door, turn the knob, and go right in. I couldn't even get into my own apartment in New York without a key.

I spotted the sewing machine and caddy right away. As I was lifting the pinking shears out of their holder, I noticed some rolled-up remnants of fabric. It was the same material as my canopy and curtains. I realized why I'd never seen anything like them; Cathy had made them herself. Why hadn't she said so?

I closed the front door and began to jog to the high school.

I made my way to the home ec room with only a few wrong turns. I pulled on the door and looked into the sewing room.

Cathy was standing over a large table, pinning a pattern to a piece of plaid fabric. There were three girls hunched over the sewing machines. I wanted Cathy to look up and see me so I wouldn't have to go inside. I waited as long as I could, then raised my voice so she could hear me above the noise.

"Here are the scissors," I called to her.

The machines all stopped running at once, and everyone turned to look at me. I felt ridiculous and out of place, standing there with my wet bathing suit under my clothes, my face red from the heat. "I'm sorry I took so long. Dad has the car and my bicycle has flat tires."

"You walked?" asked Cathy in amazement, coming over to me and taking the scissors out of my hand.

"Jogged, mostly," I said. "That's why I'm a little out of breath."

I could feel the other girls looking at me; they were the girls I had met on the beach. Cathy turned to them and said, "I'd like you all to meet Lori Nichols. Lori, this is"—she nodded to each girl in turn—"Rosemary Wilson, Bette Morgan, and Gerry Ruttman."

"We've already met," I said more stiffly than I had intended.

"Oh, that's right. At the lake." Cathy was silent for a moment as if she were trying to think of something else to say. Then she turned to me. "Well, you won't have to jog home. Take my car. You can pick me up later." As she took her car keys from her purse, she said to Bette, Gerry and Rosemary firmly but pleasantly, "Get back to work, guys. We're leaving here at twelve sharp."

"I'll drive Lori home, Miss Wellman," offered Gerry. "And bring your car back."

Cathy grinned. "No, thanks, Gerry. You have work to do, and besides, I've seen the way you drive."

Rosemary, a pretty girl with short brown hair, burst out laughing, and Gerry smiled sheepishly.

"I don't mind walking," I said. "It's not that far, and I can always use the exercise."

"Exercise? You need exercise?" Gerry said in a shocked tone. "You need exercise like I need ten more pounds." Turning to Cathy, she said, "You ought to see her swim, Miss Wellman. She does flips and fancy dives—all kinds of incredible stuff."

"So do you, Gerry," called Bette, tossing her head so that her blond hair swung away from her face.

"Yeah, but I can't help it," Gerry fired back.

Cathy laughed and took me by the elbow, leading me out into the hall. "I'll see you around noon, OK?"

I nodded absently and turned down the hall. I was thinking about Gerry. She made the other girls laugh, and at her own expense. It made me wonder if they could have been laughing at her instead of at me that day on

the beach. No, I decided. Gerry had been looking straight at me and whatever she had said
had been about me. Well, I thought, there was
absolutely nothing I could do about it, so I
might as well just forget it. Pushing open the
door of the school, I headed back home.

Chapter Ten

When we got to the mall later that day, we split up. Cathy and I headed for the clothing stores while my dad wandered around by himself. I hadn't planned to buy anything. Then in one of the stores I saw a white cotton dress with lace trim. After looking at it for a long time, I finally decided to try it on. I told Cathy I just wanted to see how it looked.

"It's beautiful, Lori," she commented.

"You really think so?" I asked.

"Yes, I do." Cathy stood back a little and cocked her head to one side. "It's romantic. You should save it for someone special." She paused, then added, "I'll bet Steve would like it."

I thought about Steve, but then another, very different boy came into my mind—the boy who had come up to my car the day I had been looking at the lake. He was so handsome. I wanted *him* to see me in that dress!

I shook my head to clear it. It was no use daydreaming about a boy whose name I didn't even know.

Using some of the shopping money that my mother had given me, I bought the dress and decided to hope for the best.

"How about shoes?" Cathy asked as we walked back out into the mall. "Do you have any shoes that would go with the dress?"

"No," I said. "The only good shoes I brought are yellow flats."

"That dress calls for something special. Let's see what we can find." We spent over an hour looking. Finally I found a pair of white espadrilles edged with satin ribbon. I bought them, and we hurried off to meet my father.

We put everything in the car, then went off to see a movie and then had a late dinner at a nearby steak house. The three of us ended up talking so long that it was almost eleven by the time we left the restaurant. But I didn't mind. After the big dinner and a long day, I felt full and happy.

When we got back to the house, I went straight to my room. I hung my new dress in the closet. Just before I got into bed, I wondered if I'd ever have a chance to wear it.

Thursday was Mrs. Irman's day off, so there was no one in the house when I got up. I was cleaning up my breakfast dishes when the door bell rang.

I hope it's not a kid selling candy, I thought as I dried my hands. I never knew how to get rid of them. Opening the door, I was all prepared to say "no." Instead my mouth dropped open with surprise. It was Gerry Ruttman.

"Is Miss Wellman here?" Gerry asked a little hesitantly.

"No," I said. "Isn't she at school?"

"We weren't supposed to meet today." Gerry bit her lower lip and sighed. "You see, I'm having trouble fitting my dress, and I need help. I went by her house, but her car was gone. I hoped she might be over here."

"Do you want me to give her a message if she calls or comes by?" I offered lamely.

Gerry looked as if she were about to cry. Not knowing what else to do, I said, "Hey, look. I don't know how to sew very well, but is there anything I can do?"

Gerry's face lit up. "You'd help me?"

"Sure, if I can."

"It won't take long," she assured me. Her words tumbled out in a rush. "I've got everything in my bicycle basket. All I need is someone to help me pin and mark the back. I've just got to get this done today, or I'll never meet the deadline for entries. And if I don't make the deadline, I'll have to take home ec over."

She looked so horrified at the prospect that I had to stifle a giggle. "Get your stuff, and let's see what we can do."

"Thanks!" she yelled as she ran back down the walk to her bike. She returned carrying a canvas tote bag. I showed her up to my room.

"Your dad isn't here, is he?" Gerry asked as she peeled out of her blouse.

"No," I said.

"Good." She pulled the half-finished dress out of the tote bag and slipped her arms through the sleeves. "It's supposed to have a zipper in the back, but I don't think there's room for one, do you?"

I pulled the fabric together, and the two borders barely met. "No way." I pulled harder until the material overlapped enough for a seam. "How is it in the front?"

"Too tight," Gerry responded in a choked

voice. She slipped out of the dress and let it fall to the floor. "I guess that's that," she said despondently. "I don't have time to start over, and even if I did, I don't want to. Maybe if Miss Wellman were here, she could show me what to do. But without her, it's hopeless. I'm doomed to another semester of sewing." She made a face at the thought. "If only it wasn't a required course! Why do girls have to take home ec, anyway? Why can't we just take whatever we want to take?"

As Gerry grumbled, I picked up the dress and looked at the side seams. I turned to her. "You know, these side seams are wider than they really need to be," I said. "Maybe you could make them narrower. That would give you enough room for the zipper. The only problem is that it might be too full in the front."

Gerry's face brightened. "I hadn't thought of that. And I could use more room in the front." She took the dress from me and studied it.

"How much do you think I should let it out? And don't say 'as much as you can!' " Gerry looked at me with mock severity.

"Why don't you take both seams out, put the zipper in, and then try it on again? We can adjust the side seams after the zipper is sewn in."

"This is going to turn out great," Gerry said happily, "I just know it is." She took a seam ripper from the tote bag and began to take out the row of stitches.

"Do you have the zipper with you?" I asked.

"Yes. I brought everything." Then suddenly her face fell. "Except a sewing machine." Her shoulders slumped in defeat.

"We have one," I offered. "It was my mother's, but now Mrs. Irman uses it. It's not fancy, but it will sew a straight seam."

"Not for me it won't." Gerry rolled her eyes. "I drive a sewing machine about as well as I drive a car—pretty badly."

"Come on!" I said, encouraging her. I was beginning to like Gerry. She wasn't anything like what I'd thought she'd be.

As I got the machine and set it up, I noticed Gerry glancing shyly around my room. "This is really beautiful," she said. "I knew it would be when I saw Miss Wellman working on your curtains at school. But she didn't say anything about the bed. I never knew anyone who had a real canopy over her bed. And the ruffles, too! I wish my bed had ruffles, but I don't think they'd look very nice."

For a minute I thought she was being critical, but then I noticed the wistful look on her face. She wasn't being mean at all, I realized—ruffles just weren't her style. Then she saw the little step beside the bed, and her eyes shone with excitement.

"Do you use it?" she cried, pointing to the step.

"Sure. Try it."

Gerry put one foot on the step, then sat down on the edge of the bed. She looked overhead at the canopy. "It must make you feel like a princess," she said.

"Come on," I said, laughing. "We've got a lot to do."

For a while I sat and watched as Gerry struggled with the zipper. Twice she had to rip out the stitches and start over. She was getting more and more frustrated. It finally occurred to me that I wasn't helping her by being there, so I excused myself and told her I'd be out on the deck if she needed me.

As I went down the steps, I felt better than I had in days. It was nice to have someone over, in this house, in my room. It was good to feel at home—in Westville.

Chapter Eleven

About an hour later Gerry called, "Lori?"

"Out here," I yelled. "In the back."

She found her way to the kitchen and came through the sliding doors. "This is great," she said as she glanced around the back yard. Sitting down beside me, she handed me the dress. "I've got the zipper in. It's not the best job in the world, but it works."

"It looks fine to me," I said. "Let's see how it fits." We went back inside and up to my bedroom.

Gerry slipped the dress on. It had a scoop neckline, a gathered skirt and short sleeves. The fabric was dark blue with tiny white vertical stripes. It made her appear taller and slimmer.

"I think it's going to work," I said as I pulled the side seams together. "Hold still while I pin these seams." I reached for the box of pins and set them on the edge of the sewing machine.

"Don't stick me," Gerry warned.

"I'll try not to," I answered.

As I worked away pinning the seams on the outside, Gerry asked, "What's New York like?"

"Crowded."

"I mean what do you do to have fun? Where do you go? What are the other kids like? How—"

"Hey, wait a minute," I interrupted. "One question at a time." Then I tried to answer her questions, telling her about school and Cheri and Central Park.

"Is that all?" She sounded disappointed. "Don't you go to lots of parties and meet lots of stars?"

"I've never met a single star," I answered. "But I saw Chris Evert Lloyd once. She was in Macy's promoting tennis rackets."

"Did you buy one?"

"No. I don't really have anyplace to play tennis. It costs a fortune to play indoors, and the city courts are hard to get on. A lot of people sign up to play there."

"We play some. There are a couple of courts

behind the high school." She was silent for a few seconds before she said thoughtfully, "I guess there are just as many things to do here as in New York. I thought New York would be glamorous, but it sure doesn't sound like it. You aren't holding out on me, are you?"

"No." I laughed. My life, glamorous? Putting the last pin in place, I announced, "There. It's done. Turn around, and let's see how it fits in the front."

"It feels good." Gerry studied herself in the full-length mirror. "And it looks pretty good, too, considering it's still pinned together. Uh-oh." Her face fell. "The seams are on the outside. I can't sew them up like that. You did all that pinning for nothing."

"No, that was just to see how it fits. See, now you know how wide to make the seams." I picked up the metal ruler and held it up to Gerry's side. "Three-eighths of an inch. I think they're supposed to be five-eighths, but they'll probably hold just fine. I'll set up the ironing board so you can iron it once you've sewed the seams and put the facings on." I reached into my closet and got out my robe. "Wear this while you're working on the dress. It's a lot easier to get into and out of than shorts and a blouse."

Gerry looked at me shyly and said, "You're really nice, not at all—" She began to blush, her eyes cast downward.

"Not at all the way you thought I was?" I finished for her. "What did you think I was like, Gerry?" I asked quietly. There must have been an edge to my voice. Gerry looked embarrassed.

"We—we thought you were stuck up," she said hesitantly. Then in a rush she added, "We thought you considered us a bunch of hicks. Last summer you never spoke to anyone. We decided it was because you thought you were better than the rest of us."

"I didn't *know* you," I said, defending myself. "I'm shy. It's hard—no, it's almost impossible for me to meet people."

There were several moments of awkward silence while we stood there trying not to look at each other. Gerry finally said, "I'm sorry. We should have introduced ourselves. You were the stranger—but you always looked so cool, so aloof, so—"

"Sophisticated?" I joked. "I'm afraid not," I added with a laugh. Then Gerry and I both laughed, and the tension evaporated.

A few minutes later I went back to my book and left Gerry to her sewing. At noon I sliced some bananas, oranges, and melons and arranged the fruit on two plates. Then I got out a couple of diet sodas and called to Gerry.

"Wow!" she exclaimed when she saw the fruit salads. "You didn't have to go to all that trouble. Thanks!" She sat beside me on the deck.

"How's it coming?" I asked.

"Slowly." She sighed as she speared a piece of melon with her fork. "Sewing just isn't my thing."

"But the dress looks really good on you. Maybe you'll even win a ribbon."

"I don't think so. You should see the other girls' dresses."

We ate our salads in silence. When she had finished, Gerry turned to me. "Well, I'd better get back to it. I've almost got the neck facing in. As soon as I finish that, I'll get out of your hair. I can do the hand sewing at home." She got up, picked up her plate, and asked, "Where do you want me to put this?"

"Just leave it here. And yell when you're ready for me to mark the hem."

Gerry was right about the work going slowly. It was almost an hour later when she finally called down to me. She had the dress on when I went in, and I was really surprised at what a good job she had done. "It looks great, Gerry. Really. Now stand up straight and I'll pin it." I sat on the floor and began to turn the hem under. "Where do you want it? Above the knee, in the middle, or below?"

"Below. My knees aren't the greatest."

"Below the knee it is," I said quickly. "You shouldn't tear yourself down all the time," I told her.

"I can't help it," she said. "It makes people laugh. You're really lucky," she said suddenly, changing the subject. "You know, having Miss Wellman for a mom. She's so great."

"Yes, she is," I agreed. "But she's not my mother. She and my dad aren't even married."

"Yes, but they will be, won't they?"

"I suppose so. In fact, I hope so. But I still have my real mother back in New York, and I wouldn't trade her for anything. I do like the idea of Cathy for a stepmother, though. I already have a stepfather, you know."

"You do? What's it like to have two fathers?"

I sat back on my heels and thought about it for a minute. In a sense, I did have two fathers. I had just never considered it quite that way.

"Lori?" asked Gerry gently. "Did I say some-

71

thing wrong? I'm always putting my foot in my mouth."

"No." I smiled. "You didn't say anything wrong. And having two fathers is great when they're like my dad and Casey. I'm sure that having two mothers will be just as good."

I put one last pin in the hem. "There." I got to my feet. "I think I've got this the right length now."

"Thank goodness," said Gerry as she slipped out of the dress. "You'll never know what a relief it is to me to get this done." She looked at me seriously. "And I'm really sorry I loaded all my troubles on you and took up your whole day. You were probably planning to go to the beach this afternoon, right?"

"There's still time," I said, looking at the clock. "If you want to, that is." I could hardly believe I had invited Gerry to go swimming with me, but I was glad I had.

"Would I!" she cried, stuffing her dress and sewing equipment into the tote bag. "Just give me ten minutes to get home and change." She told me how to get to her house, then I walked her to the front door.

Gerry took one step off the front porch and turned around to face me as I stood in the doorway. "Lori," she said hesitantly, "would you do something for me?"

"Sure," I said, thinking she was still talking about the dress.

"Would you teach me how to swim? All that fancy stuff you do, I mean. There probably won't be very many people at the lake now, and I'd like to learn."

"OK." I grinned. "But it takes practice."

Gerry's face beamed. "Boy, will everyone be surprised. It's that back dive I really want to learn how to do. I was watching you that first day you were there. I told Rosemary and Bette I was going to try to do a back dive, and they thought it was hysterical. I'm sort of the class clown, as you can tell." She looked just a little bit sad.

"Well," I said matter-of-factly, "today we'll work on back dives."

"Great. Thanks a lot. You know," she added, "that's two favors you've done for me today. I'll have to think of something I can do for you."

"Well, for starters," I told her, "you can introduce me to some of your friends—especially the guys." I nudged her meaningfully.

"That I can do." Gerry threw me a happy smile as she ran down the walk to her bicycle.

"See you in ten minutes," she called over her shoulder.

I stood in the doorway for a while after Gerry left, trying to sort everything out. They hadn't been laughing at me that day on the beach. They had been laughing at Gerry. I would have felt completely relieved if I hadn't seen the hurt in Gerry's eyes. I knew how it felt to be laughed at, even if they were only teasing.

Well, I thought as I closed the door, *we'll show them all.*

Chapter Twelve

After the day that I helped Gerry with her dress, I started meeting her and Bette and Rosemary at the beach every day. At night we'd go watch the softball games or stop at Baker's for a soda and some french fries.

One night Gerry and I were sitting in a booth at Baker's, sipping sodas and talking.

"Everyone's going over to Rosemary's tomorrow night," said Gerry. "You'll be there, won't you?"

"I don't know. She didn't mention it. Is it a big party or something?"

"No, it's just a get-together. Everybody's invited. Whoever has a party just passes the word, and we just sort of gather around and talk or play records. It's nothing fancy."

"Should I bring anything? Sodas or chips?"

"No, that's OK," Gerry said. "You see, one week we meet at Rosemary's, the next at Bette's, then my house and so on. We got out of the habit when the softball games started, but some of the gang thought we ought to start doing it again."

"It sounds like fun," I said. "I hope we get around to my house before I have—" My voice caught in my throat. I think I even stopped breathing for a second. The boy from the parking lot had walked through the front door and was standing nearby, obviously looking for someone. I forgot all about how foolish I had felt that day at the beach and wished it were me he was looking for.

He had black hair, only the edges of which were visible under a baseball cap, which was pushed far back on his head. His eyes were shaded by the cap, but I recalled that they were a warm brown. As he searched the room, his eyes met mine. He paused long enough to send a shock wave through me—and then moved on.

"Good-looking, isn't he?" Gerry commented after she saw the direction of my gaze.

"Yes," I mumbled. "Who is he?"

"Tim Cortland. Want to meet him?" Gerry

waved her arm in Tim's direction, and I panicked.

"No, no!" I looked down and stirred the ice in my glass with my straw. "Not right now."

"Well, it's too late, anyway. He's gone."

I looked up then, took a deep breath, and slid down a little in the booth, trying to relax.

"What's with you, anyhow? You said you wanted to meet some guys. The best-looking guy in Westville comes in, and you turn shy. I don't get it."

"I'd like to meet him, but just not right now." How could I explain to Gerry why I didn't want to meet him just then when I didn't even know myself? He was almost too gorgeous, but that wasn't it. There was something fascinating about Tim Cortland. I wasn't sure I wanted to risk finding out that he was just a regular person. But I couldn't resist asking, "Does he live around here?"

"Sure. Just a few blocks from you. His family only moved to Westville a couple of years ago."

"I've never seen him around before." I spoke as casually as I could.

"He's taking a special class for gifted students at Iowa State. He commutes, so he doesn't spend much time here anymore."

"He looks a lot older than us," I said.

"Yeah, I guess he does. But he's going to be a senior, too." Gerry looked thoughtful. "Tim's always been kind of serious. Not boring or anything. He's really funny sometimes. I guess he's just a little more mature than most guys our age."

"Does he have a girlfriend?" I asked, trying not to sound too interested.

"No, I don't think so." Gerry's mouth curved up in a mischievous grin. "Watch out, Lori. He's a tough one to catch. I've never seen him with the same girl twice."

"Why? Won't anyone go out with him more than once?" I asked, half hoping she'd tell me something terrible about him.

"I know tons of girls who would go out with him a million times. He just never calls them again. Maybe he's shy, like you. I don't know."

"Does he go to those get-togethers you have?" I wondered if he'd be at Rosemary's the next night.

"He came to some of them last year. But he always seemed a little out of place—you know, distant. Boy, for someone who didn't want to meet Tim, you sure are asking a lot of questions about him."

Gerry clearly wanted to know why, but I

couldn't explain it. Ever since that day on the beach road, I had dreamed of meeting Tim Cortland. But now that I had the chance to, I didn't know if I wanted to meet him after all. Something in me knew he was special—so special that I wanted to keep him at a nice safe distance and admire him from afar.

I almost didn't go to Rosemary's the next night because I knew Tim might be there. I was going to tell Gerry that my father wanted me to do something at home, but she was with me when he told me he and Cathy were meeting some friends and wouldn't be home until late.

It turned out I could relax, though. Tim never showed up. But the party was lots of fun, anyway. Rosemary's family had converted their basement into a rec room, and they had decorated it with colorful posters. There were two old couches and a few slightly tattered chairs to sit on, as well as several giant pillows on the floor. A stereo stood in one corner, and a bunch of kids milled around it going through stacks of albums.

A few minutes after I got there, I spotted Steve. He came right over to talk to me. We spent the whole party reminiscing about the hours we had spent playing Monopoly and kick-the-can with the neighborhood kids when we were younger. We kept breaking into laughter as we remembered the stupid things we'd done and the trouble we'd gotten into.

"Can I give you a ride home, Lori?" Steve asked as the party began to break up.

"I'd like that, but I have the car with me tonight," I answered. I made a mental note to walk the next time.

"Well, can we get together again sometime? I don't get away from the farm very often, but I'd like to see you again."

"Sure, I'd love to. Give me a call next time you're free." I got into the car and drove home.

As I lay in bed that night, I thought about the party. It had been fun to see Steve again. He was an old friend, and I liked him a lot. But whenever I'd try to think of Steve as a boy-friend, Tim Cortland's face would appear in my mind. I just couldn't seem to stop thinking about him. Restlessly, I rolled over, fluffed my pillow, and tried to sleep.

"Aren't you going into the water?" Gerry asked after straightening her blanket on the sand. Usually we went swimming right away, but that day I had flopped down on my stomach and was resting my head on my arms.

"In a little while," I responded. "Go on ahead."

Gerry shrugged her shoulders and ran off toward the water. She splashed a lot as she ran through the shallows but when she got into deeper water, she took off in smooth, even strokes, hardly making a ripple.

I was thinking about how much Gerry had improved when I felt a prickly sensation along my spine. Someone was watching me. There were goose bumps on my arms in spite of the hot sun. I glanced over my right shoulder and then over my left. There was no one looking at me. I looked out over the water, but the sun's glare made it difficult to see anyone's face clearly.

I shivered and sat up, folding my arms around my legs. I felt as if someone's eyes were boring right through me.

"Come on in!" Gerry yelled from the pier.

I waved and jumped up, thankful for the diversion. I waded into the water until it reached my shoulders. As I was about to dive forward, I saw someone out of the corner of my eye. It was Tim, swimming toward me.

I thought he was going to run right into me,

but he stopped a few feet away. Standing on the sandy bottom, he looked over at me. "I hope you swim better than you drive," he teased. "Those waves are awfully high." He motioned to the ripples on the lake's surface a few feet away.

"I can swim," I answered stiffly, wondering what he wanted.

"Hey, I was just kidding," he said gently. "Honest."

His smile was warm, but I was still flustered. Not knowing what else to do, I swam toward the pier, wondering if he would follow me. When I got to the ladder and looked back, I saw Tim wading toward the shore.

When I reached her, Gerry was beaming from ear to ear. "What did he say?" she asked as I sat down beside her.

"He said to watch out for the waves." I didn't feel like explaining the rest.

"What?" she asked, perplexed.

"Beats me," I replied.

"He didn't ask you out?"

"He doesn't even know me, Gerry."

"Sure he does. Everyone knows everyone in Westville."

Then Gerry began to tease me. "Oh, I forgot.

You're from New York. You don't speak to strangers."

I elbowed her in the ribs, and she yelped. But I wasn't looking at her. I was watching Tim walk across the sand. He sat down on a low stone wall, crossed his arms, and gazed back out over the water to the pier. My skin began to tingle again.

"I'm ready to go back in," Gerry announced. "I've been sitting waiting for you so long that my tailbone's starting to hurt. Come on."

"OK," I agreed. "But let's go off the other side, behind the pier."

Gerry looked from me to Tim. "You're really crazy about him, aren't you?"

Instead of answering, I jumped up and ran across the pier. I dived into the water, and Gerry followed. We worked for a while on back dives. Gerry's form was improving daily. When we finally went back to our towels, Tim was gone.

Chapter Thirteen

The next week the 4-H fair started. Gerry had finished her dress at home. She was going crazy by the time the day of the dress review arrived.

"If only I didn't have to model it," she complained. "I'm going to look huge standing up there beside all of those skinny girls."

"No, you're not," I assured her. "You're not fat."

We were sitting on our deck at the picnic table, eating a sandwich before she left for the competition. Gerry stuck her legs out in front of her and looked at them critically. "I'm not fat fat, but I'm not exactly built like Christie Brinkley, either."

"Nobody is built like Christie Brinkley!" I

declared. "Quit worrying about your weight," I added. "You're a friendly, smart, likable person, and that's what counts most. Besides, they're judging the dress, not you."

"I hope you're right."

"I am," I said firmly.

Gerry had to be at the fair early, so I went later with my dad and Cathy. We got there just in time for the dress review. I could see Gerry standing in line waiting to go onstage. She had added a narrow white sash around her waist, and it really set the dress off. I managed to get her attention. When she looked my way, I pointed to my own waist and made a circle with my thumb and forefinger. She nodded, understanding, and touched the sash. Then we grinned at each other.

Gerry turned her attention back to the stage. I looked at Cathy, who was almost as anxious about the review as Gerry was. Most of the competitors were students of hers.

"You did a wonderful job helping Gerry with her dress, Lori," she said. "She really looks lovely."

"I'll tell her you said that," I replied. "But the credit is all hers. All I did was mark the dress for her."

When it was Gerry's turn to parade before

the judges, she looked as relaxed and confident as anyone else. It wasn't until they handed out the ribbons that she lost her composure. She had won second prize.

When she finally had a chance to join us, she still looked stunned. "I really won a ribbon, didn't I? This isn't a dream, is it?"

"No, it isn't," said Cathy, smiling. "You should be proud of yourself. You did an excellent job."

"Thank you, Miss Wellman. Does that mean I won't have to take home ec over?" she added anxiously.

Cathy laughed. "Yes. You've earned the credit."

Gerry clenched her fists in triumph and turned to me. "Wait for me while I change, will you?"

My father and Cathy wandered off while I waited outside the tent for Gerry. When she came back out, she had on shorts and a T-shirt. The red ribbon was pinned to her left shoulder. "You didn't think I'd leave it behind, did you?" she asked when she saw me grin. "It's the first time I've ever won anything. I may even wear the ribbon to bed."

"I would if it were mine," I said.

"Part of it should be yours. If you hadn't

helped me, I never would have finished the dress." Then she slapped her hand over the ribbon protectively. "But just try to take it away from me!"

I laughed with her, then said, "Let's wander around a little—that is, if your head isn't so big that you don't want to be seen with me."

She shook her head and took my arm. As we walked we met some of the other girls from Westville and a few boys. "Steve's over in the cattle barn, Lori," said Bette. "He told me to tell you he was there if I saw you."

"Thanks," I said. "I think I'll go over and talk to him for a while. See you guys later." I left them and made my way to the livestock area.

Steve was sitting on a hay bale near the entrance to a stall when I found him. His face broke into a huge smile as I sat down beside him.

"Sorry I can't offer you a more comfortable place to sit," he said. "There's probably a chair around here someplace, but I haven't seen one."

"That's all right. It's good just to get off my feet. And the hay is soft."

"Soft, but scratchy. The smell isn't the greatest, either."

"Well, we can't have everything. Are you showing something?"

"You don't think I'd stay here in this heat if I weren't, do you?" Steve then pointed over his shoulder to the stall behind him. "Maggie. Best heifer in the Midwest."

"I don't know much about cows, but she looks like a real winner. Are you going to auction her off after the judging?"

"No way." He cast a fond glance in Maggie's direction. "She's for show only."

I don't know how long we talked, but I was kind of glad when I saw Gerry beckoning to me from the open doorway. The heat in the barn was getting to me.

"I've got to go, Steve. Why don't you come with us?"

"I can't. It's my turn to guard the livestock. I'll be here all night. Maybe I can catch you tomorrow if you come over."

"OK. See you later."

Gerry was looking over her shoulder and beckoning wildly with her hands. I wondered what the rush was.

"Hurry up," she urged.

"What's wrong?"

"Nothing." She took my hand and pulled me along behind her as she dodged through the crowd. "Some of the guys are having a basket-ball shooting contest. I thought you might like to see it."

There was a small crowd of people gathered around the basketball stand. Gerry began to press her way past them. "I told Bette to save two spots up front," she said.

We got all the way to the inside circle of the crowd before I saw who was shooting. It was Tim.

"One more, Tim, and you win a teddy bear," said one of the boys, laughing.

I tried to back up, but there was no place to go. I threw Gerry a mean look. She didn't see it, though, because she, along with everyone else, was watching Tim. He stepped back a little, took a deep breath, and arched the ball through the air. It fell through the hoop with a soft swish. Everyone cheered.

I was standing about six feet from Tim, still trying in vain to back up, when he turned around. Looking directly at me, he asked, "What's your favorite color?"

"Blue," I said, without thinking. It wasn't my favorite color, but Tim didn't know that.

Tim turned to the game operator at the stand. "She'd like the blue bear," he said. Then he handed it to me.

I felt like a little kid. What was even worse was that I was sure I looked like one, too. I had decided to wear my hair in braids that day. "Thanks," I said nervously.

"You're welcome," said Tim very formally. The crowd started to break up, but Tim just stood there looking down at me. And I couldn't take my eyes from his.

"Tim! Hey, Tim! Come on!" one of the guys yelled.

Tim turned away and was gone before I could say a thing. I stood there, clutching the teddy bear, looking in the direction he'd gone.

"Hey," said Gerry, interrupting my thoughts. "You're going to squeeze all the stuffing out of that bear. It's only a bear, you know. It's not Tim."

I hadn't realized that I was holding the blue teddy bear so tightly. "Oh, be quiet," I said. I swung the bear down to my side—but kept a firm grip on one of its arms.

"I think we'd better find your dad. I ran into him a while ago, and he said he wanted to take us to get something to eat."

"Why didn't you tell me before?"

"I was going to. Then I saw what was going on here, and I didn't think you'd want to miss it. You're not mad, are you?" she asked sheepishly.

Yes, I'm mad, I thought. *But not the kind of mad you mean.* "No, of course not," I said. "Let's go."

"Where did you get the teddy bear?" Cathy asked when I found her and my dad.

"One of the guys won it playing basketball and gave it to me," I answered, trying to sound nonchalant. I was relieved that Gerry had gone off to the restroom. She had teased me enough about the teddy bear.

"Did Steve win it for you?" my dad asked. "I didn't know he played basketball."

"No, it wasn't Steve. Tim Cortland gave it to me." It was the first time I'd said his name out loud. It had a nice ring to it.

"Mm-mm, yes," said Cathy. "Tim was on the basketball team. One of the better players, too."

"What do you mean 'one of the better players?' " chided Dad. "He was all-state guard. I met him briefly when he came into the bank with his father. He seems like a nice boy. I didn't know you knew him, Lori."

"We met just a few days ago," I said.

"You must have made quite an impression on him," said Cathy, smiling at me.

"You have to remember, Cathy, that Lori's a very special girl." Speaking to me again, he asked, "What's Tim doing this summer? I haven't seen him around."

"He's going to summer school. And I'm not all that special." I wished they'd get off the subject. "I don't know what he's studying, though. I really haven't talked to him that much."

Just then, Gerry returned, ending the interrogation, and we all went to get something to eat.

Later that night, when we got home, I went straight to my room. I propped Tim's teddy bear on the dresser so I could see its outline in the moonlight.

Gerry and I went back to the fair the next night. Most of the gang were standing in a little group just inside the entrance. Steve was there, too. As kids began to pair off, I hoped Steve might ask me to walk around with him, but he didn't. He was telling me about Maggie and his all-night vigil when the boys who didn't have dates began to drift away.

"See you, Lori," he called as he hurried after them.

I'm afraid the disappointment showed on my face. "He probably heard about the teddy bear," Gerry said reassuringly.

"What does that have to do with anything?" I asked.

"Well," Gerry said, pausing, "It's kind of hard to explain. It's—it's sort of a courtesy the guys have. If a girl isn't going with anyone and one of the guys shows an interest in her, like Tim did with the teddy bear, the others all stay away from her until they see what happens. Kind of like having first choice."

"First choice?" I asked. I had never heard that term used in connection with people before. "How can anyone have first choice on another person?"

"Well, you know what I mean," Gerry tried to explain. "It's kind of like saying, 'I like her, guys, so back off and give me the first chance to get to know her.' "

The thought that Tim liked me was thrilling. I had thought about him so often that I should have been light-headed with happiness. But I didn't like the system; the girls didn't have any say at all! After all, I wasn't a seat in the cafeteria that someone could call

93

first choice on! No one, not even Tim Cortland, had the right to ask anyone to back off. The more I thought about it, the angrier I got.

I craned my neck, looking for Steve over the heads of the people in the crowd. I wanted to tell him that the teddy bear didn't mean a thing, nor did Tim. But I couldn't spot Steve anywhere.

"You know," Gerry said, interrupting my thoughts, "this just isn't working out at all."

"What isn't?"

"Well, just look at us. There are hundreds of people around us, but here we are, just you and me, alone. I thought that if I teamed up with you, there'd be lots of boys swarming around and I might get one of your leftovers. Instead, it looks as if *my* luck has rubbed off on you."

"I guess so." If it hadn't been for Tim, Gerry and I might have been walking around with Steve and his friends, having a good time.

I gave Gerry a wan smile and said, "Let's go home."

She shrugged her shoulders. "OK by me. There's not much doing here, anyhow." She was unusually quiet on the way home. I wasn't in the mood to talk, either. When I dropped her at her house, she said, "I think I'll have the gang over tomorrow night, so don't plan anything else."

"OK," I promised listlessly.

When I got home, my dad and Cathy were sitting out on the deck. I checked in with them and went to my room. The first thing I saw when I opened the door was the blue teddy bear.

I stared at it for a long time before I picked it up. When I touched the soft fur and looked into the glass eyes, I saw Tim in my mind. I saw his deep-set, dark brown eyes and his black hair, and I felt the same way I had when he'd handed the bear to me—confused, embarrassed, and thrilled.

I put the bear back in its spot and tried not to look at it as I got ready for bed. Perhaps Gerry was wrong about the bear, I thought. Steve might have already made plans for the evening. He *had* said, "Maybe I can catch you tomorrow", the previous night in the cattle barn. I couldn't be sure. Even though just seeing Tim made my knees weak, I didn't like the idea of anyone, not even him, having dibs on me.

Chapter Fourteen

The next day I walked downtown and met my father for lunch. He was quieter than usual, and I wondered if there was something wrong—something he wanted to talk to me about. After we had finished our sandwiches, he looked up and said quietly, "What would you think if Cathy and I got married?"

I looked at him seriously, then smiled. "If?" I teased.

"Well, we *have* discussed it, but I wanted to give you a chance to get used to the idea before we made definite plans." He grinned back at me.

I reached across the table and squeezed his hand. "I think it's terrific."

My dad's eyes misted as he covered my hand with his. "I'm glad."

We sat there in silence for a moment. Then I asked, a little bit shyly, "Since you have to go back to the bank and I have no plans, I'd like to go over and congratulate Cathy. Do you think she'd be home?"

"I think she'd love to have you come over," Dad assured me. "And she said she'd be home all afternoon."

We left the restaurant, and I walked over to Cathy's house. Hesitantly I knocked on the door.

"Just a minute," she called. The door opened a minute later. Cathy smiled when she saw me. "Lori, what a nice surprise! Come on in."

I stepped inside the tiny house. "Dad said you wouldn't mind if I came over without calling first," I said, suddenly feeling awkward. Then the words just came tumbling out. "He told me he'd asked you to marry him. I wanted to congratulate you."

"Oh, I'm so glad you're happy about it," Cathy said, looking relieved. "I feel as though we've become friends since you came here for the summer. But I have to say, I was still a little worried."

It was my turn to smile. "I can't think of anyone I'd rather have as a stepmother."

Cathy put her arm around my shoulder. "Come on. I'll get us something to drink."

We went into the little kitchenette, and Cathy fixed a couple of glasses of iced tea. Returning to the living room area, we sat down on the couch. She told me the same thing that my dad had about the wedding date—they hadn't decided yet. Then she added that she didn't want a large wedding. "I can't stand all that fuss and craziness at big weddings. We'd like to just have a few close friends and a small ceremony. And I have the most beautiful pattern for a dress."

I didn't know much about weddings, except the ones I'd seen in movies and my mother's a few years before. But I got caught up in the conversation in spite of my ignorance. Before I knew it, an hour had gone by.

I had told Gerry I would stop at her house that afternoon, so I stood up to leave. "Thanks, Cathy—for the iced tea, and for everything else." She hugged me and then walked me to the door. I left and started the long walk to Gerry's house, wishing my dad hadn't taken the car.

Gerry had just gotten home from shopping

with her mother. She was sitting on the front steps looking a little harried when I arrived.

Maybe she was running late getting everything ready, I thought, so as I sat down beside her, I asked. "Do you need any help with the party? I could go to the store for you if you want. You look as though you're worn out."

"I am. I must have covered every inch of the new mall," she said wearily. "But I'll bounce back before tonight. Thanks for offering to help, though. I've got everything taken care of. When it comes to food, I don't forget anything." She hesitated, then added, "Tim might be at the party."

"Here? Tonight? Tim is going to be here?"

Gerry looked a little embarrassed. "I think so," she said.

Then it occurred to me. "You didn't invite him, did you?" I asked. She nodded. "Oh, Gerry, you didn't say anything about me, did you?"

"No, no. I wouldn't do that."

"Then what did you say?"

"Well, you know how it is; the person who's having the party just passes the word around."

"And you made sure Tim would hear about it," I said. She nodded again.

"Lori? You aren't mad, are you? I didn't mention your name, honest I didn't. It's just that—well, since you're too scared to go after him, I figured I'd help you out."

"It's OK," I said, looking at my watch. "Hey, if you don't need any help, I've got to get going. See you later." I waved goodbye and walked down her driveway.

I started getting ready before seven. I tried on first one outfit, then another. Nothing seemed right. Finally I chose my favorite pair of jeans and a white, button-down cotton shirt with tiny pink stripes on it. It was just the sort of thing Steve would like. But would Tim like it? I shook my head to get rid of the thought.

I had washed my hair that morning. Now I brushed it until it shone. Then I pulled it back in a french braid. Finally satisfied with my appearance, I looked at the clock. It was only seven-forty-five.

I forced myself to wait until quarter past eight before setting out for Gerry's house. I didn't want to be the first one there.

As it turned out, I was almost the last one there. "Hey, what kept you?" Gerry called as I rounded the corner of her house into the back yard. "Everyone else is already here. Well, almost everyone," she added meaningfully. I knew she meant Tim.

I hadn't realized how tense I'd been until I found out Tim wasn't there yet. I felt more at ease but disappointed, too.

Picking up a soda from the picnic table, I walked over and sat down on the ground next to Steve.

"How did the judging go?" I asked Steve. "Did Maggie win anything?"

"A blue ribbon," Steve replied proudly.

"Hey, that's great. I guess that makes me a better judge of cattle than I thought I was. I told you she was a prize winner."

"Probably just beginner's luck, Lori," Steve teased.

We had been sitting there talking for a while when suddenly I heard one of the guys call out, "Tim, you made it!"

I looked across the yard and saw Tim standing there talking to some guys. Steve looked at me with a question in his eyes. "You like him, don't you, Lori?"

"Yes, I guess I do," I answered.

"More than you like me?" Steve continued.

"No, not more," I said. "Tim's different, that's all. You and I have known each other a lot longer. I thought when I saw you that night in Baker's that maybe our friendship would grow into something more."

"But it hasn't, has it?" Steve asked gently.

"I'm afraid not," I said sadly. "I'm sorry, Steve."

"Don't be sorry." He squeezed my hand affectionately. "We can still be friends, can't we?"

"Yes." I smiled. "We'll always be friends."

We talked some more, then Paul, the boy Tim had been talking to, suddenly called out, "Listen up. Tim's got a great idea. Tomorrow night, before the softball game, we're going to have a game of our own. We'll have to round up a few extra people, but that shouldn't be a problem. Can everyone here make it?" Everyone but Steve agreed to meet at five o'clock at the softball field. He was busy.

Tim then stood up, and I thought he was going to leave. But instead, he made another announcement. "There's one other thing," he said as all eyes turned toward him. "We thought it'd be fun to play in pairs, girl and boy pairs. Everyone will be responsible for finding himself a partner. And since it was my idea"—his eyes moved around the circle of people and came back to me—"I think I should get first choice."

A few of the guys cheered and made wisecracks. When the noise died down, Tim said quietly, "Lori, will you be my partner?"

The air became charged with electricity. I'm sure everyone thought that because I'd been sitting with Steve all evening, we were a couple. If that was true, Tim's choosing me was against their rules.

"If it's OK with Steve, that is," Tim continued. "How about it, Lori?"

I looked sideways at Steve, and he nodded. "All right," I said finally.

The party broke up shortly after that. I went over to thank Gerry. She gave me a questioning look and said, "We'll talk tomorrow. OK?"

I nodded and headed for my house. As I walked, I thought about the party. I knew I had been right to tell Steve how I felt. But I had no idea if I had done the right thing by agreeing to be Tim's partner.

Chapter Fifteen

When Gerry and I got to the beach the next day, Rosemary and Bette were waiting for us. They were excited about the softball game. They kept saying that playing with a partner was going to be a lot of fun. But I could tell they were all dying to ask me about Tim and Steve.

Finally Gerry spoke up. "I know this is going to sound blunt, but I'm going to ask you anyway. Why did you agree to play softball with Tim when you were sitting with Steve all night?"

"Steve and I are just friends," I answered. "We had a long talk about it last night."

"So, you're finally going to let Tim know you like him?" Gerry asked.

"I suppose I already have."

"What bothers me," Bette broke in, "is the way Tim asked you to be his partner when you were with Steve. He didn't know that you two had talked."

"I don't know why he did that, either," I said. I was sitting on the edge of the blanket, doodling in the sand with one finger. Unconsciously, I had made a capital *T*. I smoothed the sand over it before anyone noticed.

"Well, Tim's a good guy," Rosemary offered. "He wouldn't have asked you if he'd really thought you were interested in Steve."

"Yeah, Rosemary's right," Bette agreed. "What do you think, Gerry?"

Gerry, who had been quiet after her initial question, just shrugged. "How would I know? No boy's ever had to compete for my attention." She rolled over onto her stomach.

Normally, Rosemary and Bette would have laughed at Gerry's remark. That time, they didn't. I didn't, either. I tried not to laugh at her when she made fun of herself. She seldom did it anymore, but I guess it was hard for her to break the habit entirely.

"Where is everyone?" I asked, trying to change the subject. "The beach is nearly empty."

"Most of the girls are practicing up for tonight," said Bette, "playing pitch and catch."

"Or resting," Rosemary added. "So they'll be in top form."

"Well, swimming is more relaxing than anything," I said. "Besides, it's only a ball game." I jumped up and ran into the water. When the water got too deep for me to touch bottom, I dived forward and swam underwater to the pier. But I didn't climb up the ladder. Instead, I turned around and pushed off again. "Only a ball game," I had said. If only that were true!

"Hey, wait up!" Gerry called. She was swimming toward me with smooth, even strokes.

I treaded water until she reached my side. Then we swam to the end of the roped-in area together.

"In sync, now," Gerry said as we reached the rope. She dived forward and came up on her back for two strokes. Then she went smoothly into a crawl. Usually she followed me, but that afternoon our roles were reversed, and I followed her. She led me through the routine at a grueling pace.

"I'm exhausted," Gerry said when we finally got out of the water.

"I feel kind of like a wet noodle, myself," I admitted as I picked up a towel and began to dry off.

"It's getting late. I'm going to have to leave," Bette said. She gathered up her blanket and towel. "Five o'clock," she reminded us. "Don't be late."

Rosemary followed Bette, so Gerry and I decided to go home, too.

After I had showered, I sprawled across my bed and tried not to think about anything. Tim's blue teddy bear gazed down at me from the top of my dresser. I turned my head away—only to see a reflection of the bear in my vanity mirror. I closed my eyes.

In spite of all my confusing thoughts, I dozed off.

"Lori?" my dad called as he came through the front door.

I sat straight up in bed. What time was it? Dad sometimes didn't get home until after five. I looked up at the clock and saw it was four-thirty!

"I'm in here, Dad," I called back. "Getting ready for the ball game. I've got to hurry." I sprang to my feet. If only I had picked out something to wear before I'd fallen asleep!

I rummaged frantically through my drawers. Finally I settled on a pair of blue cotton running shorts and a blue- and white-striped T-shirt. I pulled on a pair of socks and my sneakers. Then I ran a brush through my hair. I didn't have time to braid it, so I left it loose.

"The ball games don't start this early," Dad said as I rushed from my room.

"This one does, and I have to play in it." Of course, I wouldn't play until the last inning. We had decided that the boys would start the game, and the girls would play only one inning. That made me mad because I liked to play. Still, I wanted to be there for the whole thing. I reached up and gave my dad a quick kiss. "I've got to run. See you later."

I dashed outside and began to jog toward the softball field.

"Here she comes!" Gerry yelled, running out to meet me as I came through the gates and headed for the infield. "What kept you?"

"I fell asleep. I didn't wake up until half an hour ago." I slowed my pace to a walk and looked nervously at the boys and girls gathered around home plate. Tim was there, and he was watching every step I took. I began to walk even slower.

"I couldn't have slept a wink if I were you," said Gerry. "Hurry up. They're choosing up sides now."

I went over to stand beside Rosemary and Bette, away from Tim's side of the plate. He seemed to be in charge, because the other guys were all turned toward him.

"OK," he said. "Everyone's here now." He looked pointedly at me. "My team is the blue team; Paul's is the red team."

They tossed a coin to see who was up first. The blue team won and elected to take the field first. My heart sank as I saw Tim put on a chest protector and a catcher's mask. Why couldn't he have played in the outfield, where I wouldn't have to handle the ball so much when I took his place? I knew I'd make a complete fool of myself if I had to catch. *Maybe that's what Tim wants*, I thought dejectedly.

Nobody scored in the first inning. There were a lot of errors because no one was playing really seriously. The girls all sat behind the backstop, cheering everyone on, even the guys on the opposing teams.

In the top of the second inning, the red team scored two runs. But the blue team came right back with two runs of their own in the bottom of the second. Tim hit a double to drive in the second run, but he was left on base when the next man flied out.

With the score tied, the guys got a little more serious about the game. Paul, the other captain, slid into third and twisted his ankle. His partner, a girl named Julie, left to get some ice to put on his foot. Time out was called while they tried to figure out who would replace Paul as pitcher for the red team. One of the other guys on the red team could run for him, but that still left them without a pitcher.

Tim was the first to spot Steve. He had just come in. I was surprised to see him. I guessed that he had probably finished his work on the farm.

"Steve!" Tim waved him over. "How about going in for Paul?"

"Sure." Steve trotted out to third base, tagged up, and the game went on. He scored on the next hit, which put the red team ahead by one.

I could feel some of the other girls looking at me, but I stared straight ahead. Were they trying to figure out how I felt about Steve? Tim? I didn't care. I was wondering who Steve would ask to play for him now that he was in the game.

Chapter Sixteen

The blue team failed to score in the bottom of the third but tied the score in the fourth. It was time for the girls to take over—and Steve was the first batter. We had planned on playing seven innings, but with the time out, we had to cut it short so that the regular game could start on time.

"Who's batting for you, Steve?" asked Tim as he picked up his catcher's gear.

I held my breath as Steve glanced over at the dugout where the other girls and I were sitting. His eyes met mine and went right on by.

"Gerry?" he asked. "Will you play for me, or are you playing for someone else?"

"Me?" Gerry gasped. I had never seen her blush until then. I jabbed her gently in the ribs and whispered, "Say something."

"Yes. I mean no. I'm not playing for anyone."

"Then get out to the plate," Tim said. "Where's my catcher?"

I trotted over to Tim and reached for the chest protector he was holding in one hand.

He frowned at me and said, "Turn around. We've got to do something with that hair." His voice sounded harsh.

Dropping the protector, he pulled my hair back behind me and gathered in the loose ends around my neck. His fingers brushed the sides of my face and the back of my neck. Chills ran down my spine. "Do you have a rubber band?"

"No," I said in a small voice.

"Anyone have a rubber band?" he asked.

No one did. "How about a shoelace? Paul, you're not going anywhere for a while. Let me have one of your shoelaces for Lori's hair."

I held my hair in a ponytail as he returned with the shoelace. He tied it quickly, our hands meeting only briefly. Then he held up the chest protector while I slipped my arms into it. He was all business as he tied it in the back.

"How's that?" he asked.

"It's a little big," I said, pulling the pad away from my body. It reached almost all the way from my chin to my knees. I wondered what would happen when I tried to squat down like a catcher. It would probably come up over my mouth.

"Try the mask," Tim said as he slipped the webbing over my head.

I pulled the mask down and couldn't see anything. The padding above the wire mesh blocked my view.

"Think you can see a ball coming at you?" asked Tim.

"See a ball?" I asked indignantly. "I can't even see you." I pushed the mask up until I could see between the wires. Tim was grinning from ear to ear. My heart turned over. He had a beautiful smile.

"If we can adjust the back so it fits like this, I can see the ball all right," I offered.

"You can't. The straps are too long," he said reasonably. Then he pulled the back of the mask as far down as he could on the back of my head and said, "Now let go and let's see what happens."

When I released the front, it slipped down over my eyes again. Then I had an idea. Reaching up to the back of my head, I pulled my hair out through the webbing so that it held the strap below my ponytail. It was awkward, but it worked.

There were a couple of hits. Gerry got a double, and Steve really cheered for her. It made me feel good. Then the next batter struck out. The inning was over with no runs scored. It was our turn at bat.

I knew Tim would have been the fourth batter up, so it was possible that I wouldn't even have to go to the plate. I really didn't want to. A crowd was beginning to gather. It was mostly the players for the regular game, but many of them were watching us.

Gerry had to pitch since that was the position Steve had taken over. She was surprisingly good. She struck out the first batter. *Come on, Gerry,* I cheered silently. *Get the next two and I won't have to bat.* The second batter got lucky and hit a double and then the third struck out, but it didn't help me. I couldn't have been in a worse position. The score was tied, with one girl on base and two outs.

"Lori!" Tim yelled, jogging over to me as I

picked up a bat. "That one's too heavy," he said. "Try this one." He picked up a different bat, but instead of handing it to me, he stood behind me. Tim put his arms around me and held the bat in front of both of us. It felt heavier than the first bat I'd picked up.

"Hold it like this, see?"

I could hear some of the crowd laughing. I felt like a fool. No one else had been given special instructions! But I also felt a warm glow— almost as if having Tim's arms around me would protect me and make me strong.

"Put your right hand over your left," Tim continued with his instructions, "then bring the bat back like this."

I was getting a little bit angry with all his comments. "I can bat," I said.

Tim dropped his arms and turned me around to face him. He put his hands on my shoulders. "Aren't you the independent one?" he asked. " 'I can drive,' 'I can swim,' 'I can bat.' Is there anything you can't do?"

That completely broke the spell he had cast over me. "I can't stand people who make fun of other people," I snapped. Then I walked over to home plate, took a couple of practice swings, and waited for Gerry to pitch to me. The girls in the outfield moved in closer. They must have been sure that I wouldn't hit the ball very hard.

I turned around to glare at Tim—and the first pitch went by me for a strike. It was all his fault. I was getting madder and madder by the minute.

Gerry let go with the second pitch. I watched it come toward the plate and swung at it viciously. The ball sailed deep into left field. For a second I just stood there, amazed.

"Run, Lori, run!" Tim called.

I rounded first. By the time I got to second, Tim had run down to third base. He was waving me on. I knew that if Bette had already scored from second the game was over, but Tim kept motioning me toward him. I ran on as hard as I could.

When I got to third base, Tim grabbed me around the waist and swung me in a circle. "We won, Lori, we won! You did it!" When he stopped spinning me around, I was about a foot off the ground with my arms wrapped around his neck.

He set me down gently and asked, "Forgive me?" There was no mockery in his tone or in his smile, only admiration.

"You tried to make me mad, didn't you?" I accused.

"Yes."

"Why?" I glared at him.

"I was pretty sure you'd hit the ball. I wanted to make sure you'd really blast it."

Now that he had put me down, I came to my senses. "I pretended it was you."

That would have crushed most of the guys I knew, but Tim just grinned and said, "It worked, didn't it?"

I shook my head in anger and turned away from him, but he caught my arm and pulled me back.

"You might have acted as if you had some confidence in me even if you didn't," I said.

"I had lots of confidence in you. That's why I gave you a heavy bat. Do you know your eyes flash when you're angry?"

"I knew it was heavy!" I said. "Even though you said it was a light one." His remark about my eyes unnerved me, but I managed not to show it.

"It's like this, Lori." Tim draped one arm around my shoulders and led me off the field. "I figured that with that heavier bat, you could get the ball over their heads. They did the rest by coming in when they saw me coaching you. Then, when you hit the ball so hard, they had to run out to get it. Our team had time to score."

I stopped suddenly, which brought both of us to a halt. "That's mean," I said, glaring at him again.

"No, it's not. It's strategy." He smiled down at me. That, plus the pressure of his arm around my shoulders, completely disarmed me.

"What if I hadn't hit the ball at all? What would you have done then?"

"Lost." Tim's hand dropped from my shoulder. "But I prefer winning," he added with a grin.

"It was only a ball game," I said. We were facing each other at one end of the backstop. The players for the next game had to walk around us.

Tim noticed them before I did. "Hey, we're blocking traffic." He took my hand and led me into the stands, where we sat down side by side. "I just don't like to do things halfway, Lori. Not even ball games. You'll get used to it."

He let go of my hand and concentrated on the game, which was just starting. I thought about how he'd said I'd "get used to it." Was it his way of asking me to go with him? No, he wasn't asking me anything. He was telling me. I wasn't sure I liked that—but I wasn't sure I didn't, either.

I looked at Tim's profile out of the corner of my eye. He didn't seem to know I was there. I wondered if he would notice if I got up and left. But I knew I wouldn't do that. Sitting beside Tim made me feel happy. I'd felt happy when I was with Steve, too, but this was different. Being with Steve was easy, relaxing. Tim was exciting.

I paid absolutely no attention to the game. My thoughts were about Tim.

"Hey, you going with me?" Tim was standing up, holding out his hand.

"Is the game over?" I asked.

"Is the game over she asks after both sides have left the field! And I put the fate of my team into your hands?" Tim was teasing me again; there was laughter in his eyes.

I had deserved that one. I laughed out loud.

We walked toward my house hand in hand, talking and walking and thinking. When we got to my house, Tim took me by the shoulders and held me at arm's length. His eyes searched mine. He drew me toward him and kissed me lightly on the forehead. Then he dropped his arms. "Good night, Lori," he said softly.

"Good night, Tim," I said, as he turned to walk down the driveway.

Chapter Seventeen

I watched Tim until he was out of sight. I had thought he might turn and wave, but he didn't even look back. I think I knew that it just wasn't his nature. He would always be looking ahead.

It wasn't until I started to get ready for bed that I realized I still had Paul's shoelace in my hair. I pulled it off and laid it beside the blue teddy bear. Even though the shoelace belonged to Paul, Tim had given it to me, so I decided to keep it. I could get Paul a new pair of laces.

The phone on my bedside table woke me the next morning. I had overslept. I reached for it groggily and picked it up before Mrs. Irman could get to the extension in the living room.

"Lori!" It was Gerry. She sounded excited. "How soon can you get over here? We've got a lot to talk about."

"Give me forty-five minutes," I said, peering through half-open eyes at the clock. "It's ten o'clock now; I'll meet you about ten-forty-five."

"Forty-five minutes?" She sounded disappointed. "I don't think I can wait that long. I've been up for hours."

"I'll hurry," I promised and hung up.

Gerry was sitting on the curb waiting for me when I got there. "Tell me what happened," she said as she was getting into my car. "Everything."

I had to laugh at her enthusiasm. "Well," I began, as we reached the highway and turned toward the park, "you saw most of what happened. After the ball game, Tim and I watched the other game, and then he walked me home."

"Did he stay at your house for a while?"

"No."

"Did he kiss you?"

"Yes," I said. "But only on the forehead."

Gerry clasped her hands in delight.

"And then he left."

"Oh, well. That's a beginning, anyway. Are you going out with him tonight?"

"I don't know. He didn't say anything about tonight. He didn't even say he'd call." That fact had been on my mind when I went to bed and when I woke up. Most of the guys I knew would have said "see you" at least. But Tim wasn't like most guys.

"Hey, what happened to you after our game?" I asked. "I didn't see you."

For a second Gerry didn't answer. I took my eyes off the road just long enough to glance over at her. She had a dreamy look on her face. "Nothing much," she said very casually. "Steve thanked me for playing with him."

I waited for the rest of the story. There had to be more. No one gets that entranced over a simple thank you.

"Then he walked me home!" Gerry exclaimed.

"That's great! Did—"

"Nothing happened." Gerry answered my question before I finished asking it. "He didn't kiss me or anything. But we did talk for a while. He's a real nice guy. Lori."

"I know he is. Maybe he'll call you." I wanted Steve to call Gerry almost as much as I wanted Tim to call me.

"I doubt it," Gerry said, but there was a hopeful note in her voice.

We didn't swim much that afternoon.

Mostly we just lay on the sand, wrapped up in our own dreams. I relived every moment of the game, even Tim's teasing, and the walk home. Gerry seemed preoccupied, too—with thoughts of Steve, I was sure.

I didn't go anywhere that night. I just stayed home and waited for the phone to ring. At eleven o'clock I gave up and went to bed. That was Tuesday.

Tim didn't call on Wednesday, either, or on Thursday. I walked by the corner where his street and mine met and looked down toward his house. His car wasn't there.

On Friday I met Gerry at the beach. She was so excited she could hardly contain herself. Then the words tumbled out of her as I was getting settled. "Steve called!"

"When?" I sat down, drew my legs up, and wrapped my arms around them.

"Last night. He wants to go out tonight. Hey, maybe we could double-date. No, on second thought, I don't think Tim's the double-dating type."

Gerry was so engrossed in making plans for her date with Steve that she didn't notice my silence. I lay my head on my arms and looked the other way so she wouldn't see the sadness in my eyes.

Rosemary and Bette were making their plans for an evening out, too. "What are you going to do, Lori?" asked Bette.

"Probably just sit around and listen to records," I said, staring out across the water. I knew she meant, "What are you and Tim going to do?" I was glad she didn't ask any more questions because I didn't want to tell them he hadn't called or come over.

When I dropped Gerry off at her house she said, "There's still time for Tim to call, Lori. It's still early." She acted a little embarrassed but continued, "I could tell from the way you looked that he hadn't called you, but I didn't want to say anything in front of the others."

Good old Gerry. I could have hugged her for her understanding, but the best I managed to muster up was a smile.

"Maybe," I said. "Anyway, have a good time with Steve."

I spent Friday evening just the way I had told Rosemary and Bette I would, listening to records, alone. On Saturday I faked a stomachache and didn't go to the beach, and on Sunday I told Gerry I thought I should spend the day with my dad and Cathy. I said that I had been neglecting them lately. I'm sure she saw through my excuses, but she didn't say anything.

My dad knew there was something wrong. "Do you feel all right, honey?" he asked as we got into the car to go to church.

"Sure," I answered a little too brightly. "I feel fine. Why?"

"You've been acting a little depressed lately. You might be a little pale; it's hard to tell with that tan."

"I'm fine, Dad. Really I am." *There's nothing wrong with me that a call from Tim wouldn't fix,* I thought. But I couldn't exactly tell him that.

Cathy met us at the church. Afterward, we went out to eat and then drove over to the mall to see a movie. My dad didn't say anything else to me, but he must have said something to Cathy. Every once in a while I caught one of them looking at me anxiously.

By Monday I'd run out of excuses not to go to the beach. When I got there, Gerry tactfully didn't ask about Tim. She must have figured that he hadn't called or I would have told her about it. And I knew it was time I admitted to myself that he wasn't going to call. I was no different from any of the other girls Tim had dated. He'd asked them out once, but never again.

Stretching out on my towel, I closed my eyes and let my thoughts wander. I was glad it was just Gerry and me for the day. Bette and Rosemary were really nice, but I knew they would ask questions about Tim that I didn't want to answer.

"We missed you yesterday," Gerry suddenly said. "Everyone was here. Even Steve." She paused as if waiting for me to say something.

"Tim, too?" I asked as casually as I could. It was the first time I'd said his name out loud for almost a week. Even saying it hurt.

"No, I didn't mean—not—oh, nuts!" Gerry exclaimed. "What I was trying to say is that Steve was with me."

I rolled over and sat up. "Oh, Gerry, that's great!" I said, feeling really happy for her.

She blushed and looked down at the sand in embarrassment. "He was really impressed with some of the things you taught me."

"You didn't do our swim routines for him, did you?" I asked, horrified. It was like showing a boy an aerobics workout.

"Of course not," Gerry said indignantly. "We raced. I remembered everything you said, and

I beat him once. And he said he'd try to get to town tonight," she added.

"Oh, Gerry, that's wonderful. I'm so excited for you. And you and Steve are made for each other."

"You mean I look like one of his—"

I shot her a dirty look before she could say "cows."

"Oops. Sorry, Lori. It just kind of slipped out. It's hard to break bad habits."

Gerry had vowed that she wouldn't make fun of herself anymore.

"What I meant," I went on, "was that you and Steve are both very friendly, warm people. You always care about how other people feel." *Which is more than I can say for some people*, I added silently. I was thinking about Tim, of course. But I realized I had no right to think that. He hadn't promised to call me or anything. I had no right to expect that he would. *He hadn't been saying good night to me when he'd kissed me on the forehead*, I thought dismally. *He had been saying goodbye.*

Chapter Eighteen

Cathy had dinner with my dad and me that night. After we had finished eating, Dad turned to me. "We're going to walk over to the softball field. Want to come with us?"

"Not right now," I said. "There's a book I want to finish. Maybe I'll come over later." They both knew it was just an excuse. I just didn't feel like acting cheerful in front of everyone when I felt so miserable inside.

After they left, I got out the book I had started reading the day before. I sat down on the swing and opened the book to the page I had marked. But as I started reading, I discovered that I didn't remember what I'd read. I had just been turning the pages and not really paying attention. I started at the beginning again, determined to keep my mind on the story.

I was still reading when the sun went down and the shadows began to blend with the night. I had to squint to see the pages.

"Don't you know that will ruin your eyes?" a voice suddenly said.

I didn't have to look up to know who it was. I would have known Tim's voice anywhere. I looked up and saw him standing on the deck with the kitchen light behind him, looking just as perfect as he had that time I had seen him in Baker's. His hands were shoved in his pockets, and he was wearing his baseball cap. I felt the same way I had felt then, too—excited and a little breathless.

Why did you come back? I asked silently. *I can get over you if you'll stay away. It's not fair of you to walk into my life and then right back out again.* But hearts can't tell what's fair and what's not. And mine was beating wildly.

I took a deep breath to steady my voice. I was glad that I sounded so calm when really I was so unsure of myself.

"Hi, Tim."

He walked over to the swing and sat down

beside me. Fingering one of my braids, he looked at me intently.

"I've missed you, Lori," he said in a low voice.

"I've been right here," I said a little too sharply. "How did you know I'd be home?"

"Your father told me where you were. I thought you might be at the softball field, so I went there first. When I couldn't find you, I asked him. He told me to come around to the back if you didn't answer the door."

Good old Dad! I thought. He had probably guessed I had been upset over a boy.

"Didn't you miss me—even a little?" Tim's tone was gentle but questioning.

"Yes, I've missed you," I admitted.

"I'm sorry for the way I treated you, Lori." Tim was suddenly very serious. "But just then I didn't have any time for anyone, not even you. My course at Iowa State just ended on Friday, and I had to spend every night studying. On Friday I started working at the gas station again. I'm on the night shift, and it always takes a day or two to get adjusted to working all night and sleeping during the day."

"You don't have to explain, Tim," I told him,

phrasing my words carefully. He didn't owe me a thing.

"Yes, I do," he protested. "I picked you to be my partner in the softball game because I wanted to get to know you. The more we talked, the more I liked you. And I just couldn't be distracted from my studies. But I like you, Lori."

I didn't know what to say.

"There's another reason I didn't call you," he continued. "I wanted to give you a chance to see Steve if you wanted to. I have a tendency sometimes to just do what I want without considering other people until it's too late."

"Steve and I are just friends, Tim. We've known each other for years."

"That's what I thought. Still, I was glad to see Steve with Gerry at the game tonight. I didn't want to be accused of stealing his girlfriend." He gave my hand a squeeze.

I don't know how long we sat there talking, but it seemed as though only a few minutes had gone by when Tim stood up, pulling me up with him. "I've got to go, Lori. By the time I get home, change, and get to work it'll be eleven."

He drew me to him, circling me with his arms and resting his chin on my head. We just stood there for a minute or two. Then he tilted my chin up and kissed me gently on the lips.

He stepped back and let his arms drop loosely around my waist. I looked up into his dark eyes.

"I'm glad you came over," I said shyly.

"Good night, Lori. I'll see you soon— tomorrow if I can."

"Good night, Tim," I said, my heart still beating wildly from his kiss.

Tim left by the gate in the fence. I didn't go inside right away, wanting instead to sit on the swing by myself in the dark, quiet garden.

Finally I realized that it was late. My father and Cathy had probably gotten back hours ago. I got up and went into the house. "Dad!" I called as I passed through the kitchen.

"We're in here, Lori." His voice came from the living room. I found them watching an old movie on TV. "I wasn't sure it was safe to come outside," he said, his eyes twinkling.

"It would have been," I said. Then I smiled. "But, thanks, Dad."

He just smiled back, but the worried look was gone. I knew he could tell from the glow on my face that whatever had gone wrong was all right now.

*　　*　　*

Tim came over the next evening and the night after that, too. In the weeks that followed, we spent as much time together as we could. Most of the evenings we spent at my house, sitting on the swing and talking. We found that we had a lot in common; we both loved mystery novels, Tina Turner, and the New York Yankees. And Tim's parents had also been divorced, although unlike me, he had two sisters and a stepbrother.

Sometimes at night we would walk over to the field and watch one of the games. I tried to concentrate on the action on the field, but I was too aware of Tim sitting next to me, holding my hand, to really watch carefully. One night Tim looked over at me during the third inning, smiled, and said, "Let's go get some ice cream, Lori."

I agreed, but as we left, I said, "I thought you wanted to see the game."

"How could I watch the game and keep an eye on you, too? Every guy in the place was staring at you," he teased. "I did it for your own protection."

I gave him a gentle shove and pushed him off the curb. "You're selfish, that's what you are, downright selfish." I tried to sound offended.

"You've discovered my fatal flaw."

We both laughed, but I knew why we had left the game. The summer was going to be over soon, and we had too little time together to spend it with a crowd.

Whenever Tim had a day off, we went to the beach in the afternoon. We always sat with Gerry, Bette, Rosemary, and the rest of the gang. One day we were lying on our stomachs on the blanket, our faces toward each other. Our hands were down at our sides, touching lightly. I thought Tim was asleep, and I was listening idly to the chatter from the others.

"How come you girls haven't had any more parties?" Paul asked.

"There's too much to do in the summer for that," said Bette. "We'll start them again next winter."

"Then how come you had them before? There was just as much to do a month ago as there is now."

"Yeah, I guess you're right," said Rosemary. "But we see each other almost every day, either down here or at the ball games. Why bother?"

"Everyone knows everyone else, now, anyhow," Gerry said. I opened my eyes to see if she was looking at me. She was. Then I knew that the two parties had been set up so I could meet everyone. I suppose that if Tim hadn't shown up at the second party, there would have been a third one.

When I glanced back at Tim, his eyes were open. He winked at me and squeezed my hand. For just a second, I wondered if Tim had set up the softball game so he could meet me. But then I realized it didn't matter. He would have come to me when he was ready, party or no party. Just the same, I gave a silent thanks to Gerry and Rosemary for helping things along.

I tried not to think about the end of summer and having to go back to New York. Time was passing quickly. When I got a letter from Cheri, I knew I had to start thinking about leaving Westville.

"When are you coming home?" she had written. "You said you'd try to get home early, and I can't wait to see you. I've got lots to tell you."

I've got a lot to tell you, too, I thought, feeling a twinge of guilt because I had hardly written to Cheri at all over the summer. I couldn't even write her about when I was coming back. I was waiting for Cathy and my dad to set the date for their wedding. I hoped that they would decide to get married while I was still there, but they hadn't said anything.

That night I brought the subject up. "Have you decided when you're getting married yet?"

They glanced at each other meaningfully. "That depends on you, Lori," said Dad.

"Me?" I asked, genuinely surprised. "You don't need me to help you decide, do you?"

They both laughed. Then Cathy spoke, a little hesitantly at first. "We'd like you to be there. If you want to, that is."

"Oh, I do," I said. "I was afraid I'd have to leave before then."

"What we thought was this," Dad began. "We'll get married in the morning, get you on a plane that afternoon, and then take a few days off before Cathy has to be back for the new school year. When does your school start?"

"September seventh."

"How much time will you need to get ready for school?"

"About thirty seconds," I said, grinning.

"Then what do you say to the thirty-first of August?" He looked from me to Cathy, who nodded in agreement.

"But when does school start here?" I asked.

"September third," said Cathy.

"But that wouldn't be fair," I said. "That would only give you a few days for a honeymoon. I could leave sooner," I offered. "Also, the thirty-first doesn't give you much time to get ready. It's just about a week from now."

"We have the rest of our lives," Cathy said gently. "And we can get ready in a couple of days."

I didn't argue. Every day in New York was a day away from Tim. There would be too many of those without adding any more.

"The thirty-first it is, then," I said. "I'm so glad you're getting married," I added, turning more serious. I looked at Cathy. "And you'll be a beautiful bride."

Chapter Nineteen

"Can you go somewhere at eight o'clock tomorrow morning?" Tim asked the next week, two nights before I was to leave. We were taking our time saying good night to each other before he went to work.

He had his arms around my waist, and mine were around his neck. I tipped my head back to see him better. "Go where?"

"I want to take you over to State. My grade should be posted, and I may need some moral support." He grinned, but I could see the concern in his eyes, even in the darkness. "Besides, I want to show you the campus."

"Sure," I said. "I'll be ready."

Tim kissed me gently and left, as he always did, without a word or a backward glance.

My dad was surprised to see me up and dressed so early the next morning. Mrs. Irman was shocked. "I'm going over to State with Tim today," I explained before either of them had a chance to ask what had gotten into me. "He wants to show me the campus, but mostly he wants to find out how he did in his summer course."

"He isn't worried, is he?" Dad asked. "I know he's been spending a lot of time with you lately. Not neglecting his studies, I hope."

"No. I didn't even meet him until his class was almost over. He's not really worried, anyway. It's just that he wants to get into their pre-med program next year. He says he'll need top grades even to be considered."

"He will. And it'll be a long, hard road after he gets in, too." Dad's voice held a note of concern—and of warning?

"I know," I said. "But Tim can do it."

I heard a car pull into the driveway. "He's here. See you later." I gave Dad a quick kiss, then hurried outside.

Tim was exceptionally quiet the whole way there. I think he was more tense than I had realized. After an hour's drive we made it to the campus and found a parking place.

"Here it is," Tim said as we stood in front of

a tall, gray building. "Wymer Hall." He took a deep breath and exhaled slowly before taking my hand in his and starting up the worn stone steps.

It was so dim inside the building after the bright sunlight that at first I couldn't see anything. Then I noticed the bulletin board on the right wall a few feet ahead of us. Tim pulled me along with him as he stepped up to it. Tacked up on it were several sheets of paper with names and grades on them.

"Which one is it?" I asked.

"This one." Tim pointed to a paper on the left near the bottom. "You look, I can't."

I started looking for the C's but didn't see Tim's name anywhere. "Are you sure?"

"They aren't listed alphabetically. They're by grade, starting with the A's. Look again."

I began reading down the column of A's: Anderson, Charles; Arnold, Margaret; Cortland, Timothy. "You did it!" I cried, hugging him around the waist. "You can't do any better than that."

"It's only a beginning, Lori, but it's a good one. Come on! This calls for a celebration."

"Where are we going?" I asked.

"Over to the student union. Let's cut across the lawn." Most of the older buildings had been built around a square that was filled with trees, shrubs, and hard-packed dirt paths. It was more than a wooded area; it was almost a forest. Tim explained that the administration wanted to clear the area for new buildings, but there was so much opposition from alumni that they had finally left it alone. I was glad they had.

"It's really beautiful here," I said as we climbed the steps to the union.

"I thought you'd like it."

Tim found a table in a corner and ordered sodas and doughnuts for us. There were a few students at the nearby tables, but not very many; the start of the fall semester was still two weeks away.

I had thought I was going to have Tim all to myself, but no sooner had we gotten settled than I heard someone behind me call, "Tim!"

"Brent! Come on over and meet Lori." A light-haired, freckle-faced boy about Tim's height had come up from behind me.

"Lori Nichols, Brent Hacker. Brent, Lori." Tim made the introductions. "Have a seat, Brent." Tim gestured to the chair across from us.

"I can't," said Brent. "I've got to run. What are you doing back here, anyway?"

"Just getting my grade," Tim said. "And showing Lori the campus."

"Don't forget to show her Martin." Brent laughed, said goodbye, and zigzagged his way through the mostly empty tables to a side door. "Nice to meet you, Lori," he called over his shoulder.

"Who's Martin?" I asked.

"Martin's a dorm." Tim's eyes sparkled. "I was going to show it to you anyway."

We finished eating and left. Tim took me to see the dorm where he wanted to live if he went to State. "I could commute," he said, "but that takes about two hours out of the day, and I don't think I'll have two hours to spare. And then there's the weather, too. The winters are really bad here, and I can't afford to miss any classes because of snowy highways."

I tried to picture Tim going into and coming out of the dorm's heavy doors. Then I pushed the picture out of my mind. I wouldn't be beside him.

We walked on. Twenty minutes and what seemed like miles later he said, "And this is Martin."

I looked up at a six-story limestone building with lots of windows. It was taller than Tim's dorm, but other than that, I couldn't see any real difference in the two. I said so.

Tim grinned wickedly. "Martin is coed. So far it's the only coed dorm on campus, but I heard they're going to change more over next year. So many people want to live here that they have to turn people away all the time."

"Have you gotten an application yet?" asked Tim.

"I have one for early-admittance," I answered absently, thinking about Broughton.

"Good. It's harder for people who live out of state to get in. Even though you live here in the summer, they'll probably still count you as a New York resident. But if you apply early, it might help."

Tim had assumed I was planning on going to State!

"Tim," I said hesitantly, "I didn't mean I had an application for State. I'm applying to Broughton." He looked a little puzzled, so I added, "It's in Massachusetts."

His face became blank, and I felt him stiffen, but he recovered very quickly. "Well, if you think I'm going to travel all the way to Massachusetts to see you, you're wrong," he said. His grin was a little lopsided. I knew that he was embarrassed, and it was my fault.

"I'm sorry, Lori," he said, dropping my hand and sticking both of his in his back pockets. "I had no right to assume you were going to apply to State because I am. Now you know what I meant when I said that sometimes I do what I want without considering what other people want. I guess this has been a real drag for you. Coming over here, I mean."

"Oh, no, Tim, never!" I said quickly. "And I'm not committed to Broughton." I wished I had kept my mouth shut. I hadn't been all that hot on Broughton to begin with. I hadn't really thought about college. I just wanted to go somewhere where I would know someone.

"Don't say any more, Lori." Tim touched my lips with his finger. "If you've already decided on Broughton, then that's where you should go. Don't ever do anything because you think it's what someone else wants, especially not if that someone is me. One of the things I like best about you is your independence, the way you fight back when you think someone is trying to put something over on you."

There was so much I wanted to say, but I didn't know where to start. Tim dropped the subject. "You're still going to get the grand tour anyway."

He slipped one arm around my shoulders

and led me around the rest of the campus, pointing out different buildings and spots of interest. His voice was light and impersonal. I might have been a distant cousin except for the fact that his arm was on my shoulder. But I loved the campus. For the first time, being a freshman seemed real.

When we got back to his car, Tim tossed the keys to me. "You drive. And if you hear sounds like distant thunder, don't worry. It'll only be me snoring."

"Watch your knees," I said as I pulled the seat forward. "I'm afraid you're not going to be very comfortable."

"I'm so tired I could sleep with my legs in a knot." Tim had worked all night, as usual, and it had caught up with him.

By driving as slowly as I could, I managed to make the trip home last an extra half hour. I don't know whether Tim was actually sleeping, but he didn't open his eyes until I pulled up in front of my house. Then he sat up with a start. "What time is it?"

I looked at my watch. "Three o'clock."

"I've got to go. I won't be able to come over tonight, Lori. By the time I get some sleep, it will be too late."

He leaned over and kissed me on the cheek.

Then, placing his fingers under my chin, he turned my face toward him and looked at me gravely.

"Tomorrow's your last night, isn't it?" He knew it was. We had an unspoken agreement not to mention it. "Let's do something special. I've already asked the day man to switch with me so I won't have to work tomorrow night. We can stay out as late as we want."

"I'd like that," I said.

"I'll pick you up at six, OK?"

I waited until Tim had turned the corner before I went into the house. I should have been happy, but I wasn't. The day at State and the time with Tim had been wonderful until I'd mentioned Broughton and almost ruined everything. I should have been more alert. I should have seen it coming. He had given me a million clues, but I hadn't picked up on them. If only I hadn't brought up Broughton!

"Tim won't be over tonight," I said when I saw that Cathy had set the table for four. Tim had planned to eat with us that night. "He had to work last night, and he has to tonight, too, so he's sleeping now."

I didn't say much during dinner. My mind

was so taken up with my troubles that I just couldn't make conversation.

"Is something wrong, Lori?" asked Dad.

"No." I started to get up and then sat back down. "Yes. Dad," I said, "I'm really confused about college. I'm not sure if I want to go to Broughton or not. What would you two think if I went to State? It would mean I might be around some on weekends."

"It would make us very happy. Wouldn't it, Cathy?"

"Yes." Cathy smiled. "We've been hoping you might decide to come here. But whatever you decide is fine; it's really up to you."

"I guess I've got some serious thinking to do," I said. I decided I wouldn't say anything to Tim until I knew for sure what I was doing. But I knew that just thinking about going to State made me feel much better.

Chapter Twenty

It was my last full day in Westville. I went down to the beach to say goodbye to Gerry and the others, telling them I would see them the following summer. Gerry promised to write and let me know how she and Steve were getting along.

Then I went home and started getting ready for my date with Tim. First I got my new white dress out of the closet and pressed it. Then I took a long, leisurely bubble bath and washed my hair. I curled my hair, too, letting some of it fall in front of my shoulders. Then I put on my dress and white espadrilles and waited.

Tim was right on time. I met him at the front door. The look in his eyes told me that all the care I'd taken to look nice was worth it.

"You look gorgeous, Lori," he said.

"Thanks. You look awfully nice yourself." Tim had on a pair of khaki trousers and a blue- and white-striped shirt. The light colors set off his tan and made his dark features look even more mysteriously handsome.

We had dinner in one of the best restaurants in the area, complete with candlelight and soft music. Every once in a while I noticed people watching us. I knew we made a nice-looking couple, as if we belonged together.

Tim asked me if I wanted to go to a movie, but I said no. I didn't want anything to distract us from each other on our last night together. He looked relieved. I knew he felt the same way I did.

After dinner we drove back to the park, but not to the lake. Instead, we went down to the campground, which was almost deserted, and sat on one of the benches by a rippling stream.

Both of us carefully avoided any mention of our trip to State. Instead, we talked about Westville, the summer, our friends.

"How come we never saw each other last summer?" Tim asked.

"Maybe we did," I said gently, "but we just didn't know it."

We ended the evening back at my house on

the swing. For a little while we just sat there looking out at the garden, and then Tim picked up a strand of my hair.

"You have beautiful hair, Lori, but I miss the braids. When I saw you that day at the fair, I thought you looked like an Indian princess. All you needed were beads and a pair of moccasins."

I felt my throat contract at his compliment. "And I miss the baseball cap." I touched his dark hair and felt the waves in it.

Tim put his arms around me and drew me close. I don't know how long we sat there, but it seemed only minutes later when Tim said, "I guess you'd better turn in. You have a busy day ahead of you."

"So do you," I said, thinking about the double shift he would have to work to make up for our night together.

I walked to the gate with him, and we held each other tightly, neither one wanting to let go. Finally Tim took me by my shoulders and turned me around so that I had my back to him.

"Close your eyes, Lori, and don't open them for thirty seconds. I don't want you to remember me walking away from you. And I'm not going to look back. I never have because I was afraid that if I did, you wouldn't be there."

I felt his lips brush the top of my head. "I love you," he whispered.

"I love you, too, Tim."

He squeezed my shoulders gently. Then his hands dropped and he was gone.

I stood there for more than thirty seconds. It took longer than that to blink back the tears.

The next morning I really had to rush. I had packed a few things the previous afternoon, but not enough. My mom would be furious at the way I stuffed my clothes in my suitcases, but I didn't have time to worry about it. I made a mental note to unpack myself so she wouldn't see what a mess I had made of everything.

I closed and locked the last suitcase. Then I saw the blue teddy bear. I wasn't about to leave it there, and I certainly couldn't get it in a suitcase. I tied Paul's shoelace around its neck and decided I could carry it on the plane.

When my dad opened the front door to carry my luggage out, I heard him say, "What's this?"

"What's what?" I went to the door with the

teddy bear tucked under my arm and looked outside.

"It's for you, Lori." Dad handed me a package the size of a shoebox. It was wrapped in gift paper, but instead of a ribbon there was a note taped in the center. It read, "Lori, Don't open this until you are on the plane. Tim."

Tim must have dropped it off on his way to work. I knew he'd had to be there by seven. For a moment I just stood there, trying to imagine what was inside.

"Lori? Come on. We're running a little late," Dad called.

I went back inside and took one last look around my room, grabbed my purse, and rushed outside.

My dad and Cathy had made arrangements to be married in the county clerk's office with just me and one of Dad's friends from the bank as witnesses. It was a brief, lovely ceremony—and we left immediately afterward for the airport.

I had my hands full with my purse, the teddy bear, and Tim's present. The flight attendant smiled when she saw what I was carrying, but she didn't say anything. She probably hadn't seen many sixteen-year-olds clinging to big, blue teddy bears but I figured she had seen lots of other strange things.

I held Tim's box on my lap until the plane leveled off. Then I couldn't stand to wait any longer. I unwrapped the package and lifted off the lid.

It was not only the size of a shoebox; it *was* a shoebox. And inside was one shoe—an Indian moccasin with fringe around the sides and little white, red, and black beads on the toe. Inside the single shoe was a note.

"I'll keep the other one for you until you can walk beside me again."

A lump rose in my throat. I hugged the moccasin to my chest.

There was one other thing in the box—a long envelope with my name on the outside.

I opened the envelope and took out a printed form. It was an admission application to State. Across the top, Tim had written lightly in pencil, "I don't give up easily."

It's hard to laugh and cry at the same time, but somehow I managed it.

I was halfway to New York when I placed the moccasin back in its box. It wouldn't be alone for long. I knew I was going back to Westville. I had to. Tim was waiting for me.

David Cameron

Class Act

Nigel Cawthorne

Dearest James,

Wishing you a wonderful
30th birthday!

[signature]

(Joe and Oven)

First published by Endeavour Press Ltd in 2015.